# Death Waits at Sundown

# SELECTED FICTION WORKS BY L. RON HUBBARD

## FANTASY
The Case of the Friendly Corpse

Death's Deputy

Fear

The Ghoul

The Indigestible Triton

Slaves of Sleep & The Masters of Sleep

Typewriter in the Sky

The Ultimate Adventure

## SCIENCE FICTION
Battlefield Earth

The Conquest of Space

The End Is Not Yet

Final Blackout

The Kilkenny Cats

The Kingslayer

The Mission Earth Dekalogy*

Ole Doc Methuselah

To the Stars

## ADVENTURE
The Hell Job series

## WESTERN
Buckskin Brigades

Empty Saddles

Guns of Mark Jardine

Hot Lead Payoff

A full list of L. Ron Hubbard's
novellas and short stories is provided at the back.

*Dekalogy—a group of ten volumes

# L. RON HUBBARD

# Death Waits at Sundown

GALAXY
PRESS

Published by
Galaxy Press, LLC
7051 Hollywood Boulevard, Suite 200
Hollywood, CA 90028

Printed in the United States of America.

ISBN-10 1-59212-400-3
ISBN-13 978-1-59212-400-8

Library of Congress Control Number: 2007903535

# Contents

# Stories from Pulp Fiction's Golden Age

AND it *was* a golden age. The 1930s and 1940s were a vibrant, seminal time for a gigantic audience of eager readers, probably the largest per capita audience of readers in American history. The magazine racks were chock-full of publications with ragged trims, garish cover art, cheap brown pulp paper, low cover prices—and the most excitement you could hold in your hands.

"Pulp" magazines, named for their rough-cut, pulpwood paper, were a vehicle for more amazing tales than Scheherazade could have told in a million and one nights. Set apart from higher-class "slick" magazines, printed on fancy glossy paper with quality artwork and superior production values, the pulps were for the "rest of us," adventure story after adventure story for people who liked to *read*. Pulp fiction authors were no-holds-barred entertainers—real storytellers. They were more interested in a thrilling plot twist, a horrific villain or a white-knuckle adventure than they were in lavish prose or convoluted metaphors.

The sheer volume of tales released during this wondrous golden age remains unmatched in any other period of literary history—hundreds of thousands of published stories in over nine hundred different magazines. Some titles lasted only an issue or two; many magazines succumbed to paper shortages during World War II, while others endured for decades yet. Pulp fiction remains as a treasure trove of stories you can read, stories you can love, stories you can remember. The stories were driven by plot and character, with grand heroes, terrible villains, beautiful damsels (often in distress), diabolical plots, amazing places, breathless romances. The readers wanted to be taken beyond the mundane, to live adventures far removed from their ordinary lives—and the pulps rarely failed to deliver.

In that regard, pulp fiction stands in the tradition of all memorable literature. For as history has shown, good stories are much more than fancy prose. William Shakespeare, Charles Dickens, Jules Verne, Alexandre Dumas—many of the greatest literary figures wrote their fiction for the readers, not simply literary colleagues and academic admirers. And writers for pulp magazines were no exception. These publications reached an audience that dwarfed the circulations of today's short story magazines. Issues of the pulps were scooped up and read by over thirty million avid readers each month.

Because pulp fiction writers were often paid no more than a cent a word, they had to become prolific or starve. They also had to write aggressively. As Richard Kyle, publisher and editor of *Argosy,* the first and most long-lived of the pulps, so pointedly explained: "The pulp magazine writers, the best of them, worked for markets that did not write for critics or attempt to satisfy timid advertisers. Not having to answer to anyone other than their readers, they wrote about human beings on the edges of the unknown, in those new lands the future would explore. They wrote for what we would become, not for what we had already been."

Some of the more lasting names that graced the pulps include H. P. Lovecraft, Edgar Rice Burroughs, Robert E. Howard, Max Brand, Louis L'Amour, Elmore Leonard, Dashiell Hammett, Raymond Chandler, Erle Stanley Gardner, John D. MacDonald, Ray Bradbury, Isaac Asimov, Robert Heinlein—and, of course, L. Ron Hubbard.

In a word, he was among the most prolific and popular writers of the era. He was also the most enduring—hence this series—and certainly among the most legendary. It all began only months after he first tried his hand at fiction, with L. Ron Hubbard tales appearing in *Thrilling Adventures, Argosy, Five-Novels Monthly, Detective Fiction Weekly, Top-Notch, Texas Ranger, War Birds, Western Stories,* even *Romantic Range.* He could write on any subject, in any genre, from jungle explorers to deep-sea divers, from G-men and gangsters, cowboys and flying aces to mountain climbers, hard-boiled detectives and spies. But he really began to shine when he turned his talent to science fiction and fantasy of which he authored nearly fifty novels or novelettes to forever change the shape of those genres.

Following in the tradition of such famed authors as Herman Melville, Mark Twain, Jack London and Ernest Hemingway, Ron Hubbard actually lived adventures that his own characters would have admired—as an ethnologist among primitive tribes, as prospector and engineer in hostile climes, as a captain of vessels on four oceans. He even wrote a series of articles for *Argosy,* called "Hell Job," in which he lived and told of the most dangerous professions a man could put his hand to.

Finally, and just for good measure, he was also an accomplished photographer, artist, filmmaker, musician and educator. But he was first and foremost a *writer,* and that's the L. Ron Hubbard we come to know through the pages of this volume.

This library of Stories from the Golden Age presents the best of L. Ron Hubbard's fiction from the heyday of storytelling, the Golden Age of the pulp magazines. In these eighty volumes, readers are treated to a full banquet of 153 stories, a kaleidoscope of tales representing every imaginable genre: science fiction, fantasy, western, mystery, thriller, horror, even romance—action of all kinds and in all places.

Because the pulps themselves were printed on such inexpensive paper with high acid content, issues were not meant to endure. As the years go by, the original issues of every pulp from *Argosy* through *Zeppelin Stories* continue crumbling into brittle, brown dust. This library preserves the L. Ron Hubbard tales from that era, presented with a distinctive look that brings back the nostalgic flavor of those times.

L. Ron Hubbard's Stories from the Golden Age has something for every taste, every reader. These tales will return you to a time when fiction was good clean entertainment and the most fun a kid could have on a rainy afternoon or the best thing an adult could enjoy after a long day at work.

Pick up a volume, and remember what reading is supposed to be all about. Remember curling up with a *great story*.

—Kevin J. Anderson

KEVIN J. ANDERSON *is the author of more than ninety critically acclaimed works of speculative fiction, including* The Saga of Seven Suns, *the continuation of the* Dune Chronicles *with Brian Herbert, and his* New York Times *bestselling novelization of L. Ron Hubbard's* Ai! Pedrito!

# Death Waits at Sundown

# Chapter One

L YNN TAYLOR rocketed into Pioneer leaving a hurricane of dust in his path. He skidded his buckskin stallion to a stop before the sheriff's office and leaped down to stride with loud boots up the steps and through the door.

Pioneer's denizens had been startled at his abrupt appearance. The men in the sheriff's office stared at Lynn and then shot questions at each other.

Lynn Taylor's square jaw was set and his eyes were chunks of ice. His batwings were thick with the mud and dust of long travel and his stubble growth of beard was whitened with alkali. But on each thigh there gleamed clean guns, tied down—and those guns and thongs meant Texas.

"Which one of you gents is McCloud?" said Lynn Taylor, dropping his quirt with a crack upon the desk.

The man behind it sat forward with a humorless, confident grin and pushed his white sombrero up from his sweaty brow. "I'm McCloud." And his stare plainly said, "What are you going to do about it?"

"I'm Lynn Taylor. Where's my brother?"

McCloud leaned back again, though the others in the room were still tensed and wary. "He's where he belongs, fellah. You wasn't thinkin' of doin' anything about it, was you?"

3

"I kind of had that in mind," said Lynn, scanning the others in the room and labeling them as hard cases. "When is the trial?"

McCloud laughed easily. "Looks like your information come late, Taylor. The trial's over and Frank Taylor swings tomorrow at sundown."

"Maybe," said Lynn, looking McCloud over. "I'm askin' to see him."

McCloud hesitated and then he shrugged. "All right, Texas. Can't be any harm in that. But get this straight. The vigilantes has things in hand—*and we don't want no outside interference.*"

He got up and took a ring of keys down from the wall. Two of the others stood and swaggered carelessly after the big Texan. It was dark in the cells. Ahead a cot creaked and Frank Taylor rose to eye the coming party with suspicion.

Worry and two weeks of confinement had thinned and blanched his young face. His young body was braced and surly as he waited for the head of the vigilantes. And then he gave a glad start. "Lynn!"

"Think I'd leave you in the lurch?" said the Texan. "Open it up, McCloud. I want a talk with the kid."

"You say what you've got to say right here in my presence," stated McCloud. "We didn't go to all the trouble of pickin' up this precious brother of yours just to let him get away from us again."

Lynn barely glanced at the vigilante chief. He moved up to the bars. "I came as soon as I got your letter, kid. What are they doin' to you?"

4

"It's a frame!" said Frank Taylor. "I'm here because I was sap enough to build up my spread to a point where somebody else wanted it. I'm a fall guy for a set of jobs I never pulled. You got to believe me, Lynn. I didn't rob nothing. If you want to see the guy that did it, turn around and look."

"Shut up," said McCloud. "Nobody'll listen to a lie like that."

"They'd listen if they weren't scared of you!" said Frank. "Lynn, you got to set this thing to rights. I swing tomorrow night. I didn't do a thing!"

Lynn looked at the eager, pleading face of his younger brother. "Sure, I know that, kid."

"Time's up," said McCloud uneasily.

"Don't worry about anything, kid," said the Texan, touching the hand on the bars very briefly. He turned and walked back along the corridor, the outer cell door clanging behind him.

In the office again, McCloud looked carefully at Lynn. "Listen, Texas, I wouldn't advise you to start anything. You ain't got any friends in Pioneer."

"Have you?" said Lynn meaningly.

McCloud laughed. "Ask around. Your brother is full of locoweed. He stopped the Overland seven times and took the weight off its springs. The last time he killed the driver. And plenty of cows have turned up missing since he started to increase his spread. I might," he added, "go as far as to say that a Taylor would show good sense if he pulled out of Pioneer—tonight."

"Yeah?" said Lynn.

"Yeah," said McCloud.

5

"Thanks for the advice," said Lynn. He casually inspected the five gunmen who lounged in chairs around the walls and each returned his stare silently.

Lynn walked out, conscious of the eyes on his back. He took his buckskin's bridle and led him toward the Silver Dollar Stable for a well-earned rubdown and feed of oats.

The stableman offered to take the rein but Lynn withheld it, preferring to stall the buckskin himself. Glitter, though tired from the wearing ride, might still have enough energy left to make mincemeat out of a careless hostler.

Lynn poured a can of oats into the manger and went to work with sponge and brush. He was so deep in thought that he was startled when a stranger spoke behind him.

"You're Lynn Taylor, ain't you?"

Lynn turned to see a weather-beaten, sun-dried westerner whose leather vest bore evidence of having had something pinned over the heart.

"I'm Hawkins," said the stranger. "Six weeks ago I was the sheriff around here—but that was before McCloud and his crowd began to yell for law and order and got the townspeople behind them. If I don't make a mistake, Taylor, you're thinkin' of doin' something to keep them from stringin' up your brother."

"Yeah, I did have some dim idea along those lines," said Lynn, continuing his work.

"I've heard of you," said Hawkins.

Lynn stabbed a questioning glance at the old man.

"We hear about most of the Texas gunfighters here in

Arizony," continued Hawkins. "But I didn't think you'd get here in time. As it is, you're too late even now. You couldn't break him out. There are fifteen men, all of them good, on that damned vigilance committee. I mean good with their guns. And McCloud's got a reputation up north. He'll own Pioneer in another month and the fools around here yell their heads off for him. Y'ain't thinkin' of standin' up and blazin' it out with him, are you?"

"Maybe."

"Look, Taylor, I ain't tryin' to be nosy. It's good business for me to give you a hand. I don't rate in this place now. So many crimes came off while I was in office that it took two clerks to file the reports on them."

"And you couldn't stop them from happening?"

"Takes more than one old man with a gun to stop a man like McCloud. If you and me teamed up, maybe I could get my job back and remove McCloud's danger to this town."

Having finished the rubdown, Lynn wiped his hands and then extended his right to Hawkins. "Okay, but you got to do things my way. That all right?"

"Well . . ."

"Why hesitate?"

"I've heard your reputation, after all."

"You never heard of me shootin' a man in the back, Hawkins."

"That's so."

"And if you don't think I'll move heaven and earth to keep my kid brother from swingin', you're crazy."

"What's your idea?"

"Is there a stage coming in here tonight?"

"One due at eleven o'clock."

"Will it have anything on it?"

"Regular dispatch box. Maybe two—three thousand. Say, Taylor, you must be loco! How could that help your kid brother?"

"Never mind that. The point is, are you willing to help me rob that stage if there's no shooting?"

"If . . ."

"You're either with me or you're not. You want your job back and unless I get killed in this bargain, it's yours. Are you going to help me rob that stage or ain't you?"

"All right," said Hawkins, doubtfully, "but by God, I never thought I'd have to commit robbery to establish law and order."

# Chapter Two

AT nine o'clock, Lynn Taylor met Hawkins on the corner by the bank where the shadows were deep. The street was streaked by lights from the saloon windows and the whirr of wheels was commingled with tin-panny pianos and half-drunken arguments.

Lynn looked at the gallows which had been built in the town square and gave a slight shudder. Against the palely rising moon the indistinct silhouette was easily imagined to already hold its prey. That very afternoon had seen the completion of the thirteenth step.

"I'll starve that thing or go down tryin'," said Lynn, half to himself. "Why the hell do men get such ideas, Hawkins?"

"Well, there's such a thing as law and order, Texas. Or maybe you ain't heard."

"Law and order?" spat Lynn. "You ready to high-tail it?"

"Now look," said Hawkins, "I ain't exactly squeamish but if McCloud ever gets an idea who done this thing, he'd hang us too. 'Course it's a good idea. If there's a robbery while your kid brother is in jail, then it'll look fishy that he done the others. But maybe ever'body will see through that."

"We're takin' a chance," said Lynn. "By the way, is that 'dobe house across from the gallows there where Fanner McCloud lives?"

9

"Yeah."

"Okay, let's go. You get a couple horses off that hitchrack . . ."

"My God!" said Hawkins in alarm. "You ain't goin' to steal horses too!"

"Why not? My buckskin needs a rest. If you won't then here I go."

And he suited action to the word and returned shortly leading a dun and a roan whose owners were getting loudly drunk in the Diamond Palace Saloon.

Hawkins mounted with misgivings. But if the truth be known he was a little frightened of this nerveless, ice-eyed devil who had blown in from the tumultuous south.

An hour later they were deep in the darkness of a canyon along which ran the stage road to Pioneer. The wind was soughing lonesomely through the scrub pines and far off an owl added his mournful dirge to the spooky scene.

Hawkins shuddered. "What do you want me to do?"

Lynn glanced at a tall black rock which loomed over the roadway. "I'm going up there. You stand easy in that clump of brush ahead and once I drop on the stage, you swerve in and pull in the lead hosses. And don't miss because we don't want no runaway."

"All right," said Hawkins faintly.

Lynn hid his mount in a patch of trees and then crept up to the top of the tall rock. He lay down to watch the road to the east.

The wind whispered and rustled his neckerchief and the owl, scenting trouble, soared away on silent wings to hoot one final time in the dim distance. After that it was quiet. Lynn could see nothing of the ex-sheriff and could only hope that the man would do his appointed job. Otherwise there might be trouble. This road was narrow and at the curves the drop into the stream below was something close to a hundred feet.

Pondering over his future courses to keep from getting too tense with waiting, Lynn passed the time. At long last he heard a rumble of wheels and the rhythm of hoofs and jingle of harness. In a few minutes the headlamp of the stage jogged into view. Because of the treacherous road the driver was taking it easy. The messenger was almost asleep, gun loosely against his chest and chin down.

Lynn crept to the very edge above the road. The lead horses passed under him. Then the next team and the third. The moment had arrived. With the box just below him he leaped. For an instant he felt that he had waited too long and would hit the road. But before the thought was wholly formed his boots slammed against the top of the stage and he lunged for the backs of the two men.

The instant he struck, training made the messenger whirl about. He was in no position to use his gun except for a butt thrust. He stabbed hard. Lynn snatched the weapon and pulled. He stood the messenger straight up and before the man would let go, Lynn sent a right crashing to his jaw. The fellow staggered, relinquishing his hold to grab for his assailant.

The driver, hands full of reins, sent a white-eyed glance at Lynn and sought to disentangle a hand so that he could draw.

Lynn had the messenger's coat front and the fellow flailed with wild fists while they tottered on the precarious footing.

*Lynn snatched the weapon and pulled. He stood the
messenger straight up and before the man would let go,
Lynn sent a right crashing to his jaw.*

Letting go with one hand, Lynn took aim. His blow was perfect. The messenger went limp and Lynn dropped him down to the confinement of the baggage rack.

By this time the driver was ready, all reins in one hand, foot hard on the brake and fingers wrapped around his Colt. He almost completed the draw before Lynn seized him and flung him outward over the rocky ground. The man strove to save himself and the Colt clattered to the dusty road. Lynn snatched him back again and banged his head against the edge of the seat. The driver sighed and relaxed. Lynn straightened him out.

It was the work of a moment to shoot the dispatch box off and into the dirt.

Hawkins had the heads of the lead team and had brought them to a quiet stop.

Lynn signaled with a wave of his hand. The driver was coming back to life and Lynn wasted no time. He dropped to earth, scooped up the box and sprinted up the slope to his waiting horse. He forked leather and dug spur to race down the bank toward Hawkins, who was already moving rapidly away.

Behind them a passenger sent a wild shot with a hopeful oath. The messenger came around and pumped his magazine empty. But Lynn and Hawkins were gone.

Lynn stripped the bandana from his face and flung it to the trail. He laid on with his quirt.

"I hope you know what you're doin'," said Hawkins. "Men have hung for less than this."

"I hope I do too," said Lynn.

"You mean you ain't sure?"

"Is anybody ever sure of anything? Come on, fellah, ride or them delirium tremens of yours'll come true for certain."

An hour later, Hawkins and Lynn Taylor were part of the astounded crowd who heard the driver's lurid tale of the holdup.

"An' so I shoots at him point blank but he just laughs at me. He beats me over the head with his gun and grabs the box. . . ."

Lynn grinned a little to himself.

Somebody in the crowd said, "Hell, is that goin' to start all over again? I thought we had the ringleader."

McCloud was on the high boardwalk before the saloon, his narrow face half alight from the oil lantern on the stage. "It's some of his pals, that's all. Don't get nervous, gents. We got the situation in hand. And when they see us hangin' Frank Taylor, they'll know we mean business."

"Who do you think done it?" said somebody else.

"I got my ideas," said McCloud, looking down at Lynn who stood by the stage wheel.

Hawkins whispered, "Maybe we better beat it. He's got men enough to do anything he wants and . . ."

"Shut up," said Lynn. "You'll play this thing through or I'll tip McCloud it was you."

"You wouldn't!" gasped Hawkins.

"Sure I would," said Lynn with a pleasant smile. "Now take it easy."

"Sure. Sure," said Hawkins, his teeth beginning to chatter. "Sure, I'll take it easy."

# Chapter Three

AT two o'clock the following afternoon, Lynn Taylor sat at the window of his hotel room and watched ranchers and their riding crews pour into Pioneer for the hanging. They came to make a holiday of it and as one outfit greeted another, cliques began to form while men swapped their experiences since last meeting. Here and there fights started, to be quickly stopped. Along the high boardwalks men stopped to argue about the hanging and from snatches of conversation which floated up from the walk, Lynn found that the country was divided upon the guilt of Frank. Those few who had known him well were loud and vociferous in their declaration of its impossibility. But in the main, blinded by lust for "justice" and carried forward now by mob spirit, cattlemen began to applaud McCloud's swift stopping of the crime wave, damning the apparent incompetence of Hawkins in the same breath.

A few discussed the holdup of the night before and McCloud went about dropping remarks that he knew the guilty party. He preferred to act wise and mysterious about it and was quite successful in creating face by the attitude.

Lynn heard the door open behind him and whirled, hands darting to his guns. But it was Hawkins. He came swiftly through the room and to the point.

"Taylor, you've got to get out of here. Somebody's got the idea that you pulled that stage job and, after all, you did. If you don't take it on the run, there's goin' to be two gibbets decorated instead of one."

"Fanner McCloud knows where to find me."

"Yeah, but Fanner McCloud's no fool. He knows it'll cost somethin' to pick you off. Frank wasn't such shucks as a gunman. Maybe McCloud figures that if you're in the crowd when they start to hang Frank, he can sing out and you'll have so many around you you won't have a chance to get away."

"Yeah. Maybe so. Did you get my note to Frank?"

"Sure. He's standin' up under it pretty good. God, but that kid sure has got faith in you, Texas. Before you came he was half out of his head but now he's quieted down. He says, 'Tell Lynn I ain't worryin' none now.'"

Lynn turned back to the window and looked up the street toward the buying pens where cattle were bought for the north trailing. About fifty head of longhorns were there now, restless with all the noise of the town.

"Maybe it isn't very smart to stay around," said Lynn.

"Now you're talkin'," said Hawkins.

Lynn stood up and tightened the thongs on his thighs. He took out his guns and gave each cylinder a spin to check the loads. Giving them a border roll, he slipped them into their holsters.

Hawkins did not trail him very far, parting from him at the back of the hotel. Lynn was amused at Hawkins' reluctance to be seen with a marked man.

16

The livery stable was three buildings down the street and Lynn leisurely made his way toward it. He entered the pungent interior from the rear and looked around. Seeing nothing out of order he approached Glitter's stall. He was so deep in thought that he sensed rather than heard the swish of a rope.

He spread out his arms and ducked. But he was too late. The man in the loft had made a true cast and with a jerk he brought Lynn's arms to his sides. Even then Lynn made a stab at his guns but the rope pulled him off his feet.

On his knees in the straw, he glared with angry eyes at the two who stepped watchfully from an empty stall. They were McCloud's men. The other in the half-loft dropped down into a broken bale and took up his lariat slack as he approached his captive.

One of the others went back of Lynn and flipped the guns away, thrusting them into his waistband. He turned to saddle Glitter but the stallion had other ideas which he expressed with a slashing kick. The fellow withdrew hastily.

"Saddle your own, Texas."

The man with the rope eased up. Slowly Lynn did as he was told. Three other mounts were led from their stalls already saddled.

"Are we going places?" said Lynn.

"Think we want a lynch mob to spoil this hangin'?" said a fellow with reddish eyes and a discolored mustache. "We got law an' order around here and you ain't goin' to mess it up. You're goin' to have a legal trial tomorrow when things quiet down and then we're goin' to hang you."

"That's tellin' 'm, Stew," said the man with the rope.

"I get it," said Lynn. "When there ain't so many in town to see what you call justice. Mind tellin' me what for?"

"For robbin' the stage last night, that's what for."

"After the driver leaves. Is that it?" said Lynn.

"Maybe there's such a thing as bein' too smart," said Stew.

"I heard somethin' said about somebody findin' a neckerchief on the road with an 'M' on it," said Lynn.

Stew looked uncertain. "That don't prove nothin'."

"It did to the driver and you've had him dead drunk ever since."

"C'mon," said Stew, impatiently. "We ain't got all day."

Lynn mounted up, shedding the rope. The cavalcade headed for the front of the stable.

"Don't try nothin' fancy," warned Stew. "Just ride east like nothin' was wrong. If you make a break, we'll find plenty of reason to plug you. Get goin', Texas."

They went into the brilliant sunlight of the street and in the press of horsemen who still continued to come into town, the three riders following close on the heels of one were scarcely noticed.

At a trot, Lynn headed for the open country, his three guardians staying close to him.

"You mind tellin' me where we're goin'?" said Lynn, over his shoulder.

"To Fanner's ranch, if you got to know. An' we don't like missin' the hangin' any more than you do."

For five miles, Lynn proceeded with a great docility which

gradually lulled the watchfulness of his captors. They were going through a heavily wooded pass which led to a plain beyond and it was necessary to duck to avoid being brushed out of the saddle by pine boughs.

They were in single file now, Lynn still ahead for the reason that the men disliked riding with their backs to him. They rounded a bend in the thickly shrouded trail and for a brief instant, Lynn was masked from the rest. And in that instant he did two things. He dug spur to the buckskin and grabbed a bough over his head, swinging up, sent by the surge of his mount.

With a startled snort, Glitter charged away. The sound was enough to send three sets of spurs driving home. Heads down to miss the swinging bough, the trio dashed ahead.

Stew was the last in line. A bomb dropped on him, knocking him out of the saddle. A hand crushing against his mouth stifled any sound he might have uttered. His mount raced on, still furnishing hoofbeats to assure the others.

Lynn was up first. He yanked Stew to his feet and slammed him down again with a solid blow to the jaw. Stew grunted and twisted into a ball and then lay still.

With a quick movement Lynn retrieved his guns out of Stew's belt and holstered them.

Ahead the others broke into the open and were astounded to see that they pursued a riderless horse. They looked back to find a riderless mount behind them and with a yell they pivoted and charged again into the woods.

Lynn stood in the center of the trail. The first saw him and

19

drew. The second pulled up and chopped down. Four shots sounded almost as one. And smoke rolled from the muzzles of Lynn's guns.

He holstered them quietly and placed his fingers in his mouth to whistle. Glitter came in a moment, stepping gingerly around the two things on the trail and giving the nervous, masterless mounts a disdainful glance.

Lynn glanced at the sun. The shadows were very long and he had five miles to go.

Swinging up, he dug spur, and with Glitter's hoofs kettledrumming a mad staccato, raced through the hills toward Pioneer.

# Chapter Four

McCLOUD had appointed himself hangman, being less squeamish in such matters than other men. He was well aware that he made a fine showing there on the gallows platform with all the country gathered in the street and square about it.

From the jail came a tight group of vigilantes, forming a square around the prisoner. The crowd gave way. Here and there somebody jeered, but the jeers lessened into undertone expressions of wonder. The prisoner was not at all downcast. Though he had a hard, Texas way about him at all times, Frank Taylor was bright of eye and he unceasingly looked at the people he passed as though a word of greeting was ready on his lips. He was completely detached from his role of a doomed man. The attitude was variously interpreted as nerve and callousness but McCloud, with an inward grin, was confidently in possession of Frank's hope and its disaster.

Solemnly the guards marched their captive up the thirteen steps and each step the prisoner's boot touched gave forth a hollow, dismal sound which echoed across the silent crowd.

When Frank reached the platform, the new planks creaked and that sound too was abnormally loud. A few in the crowd found their voices and yelled but they too fell silent after a moment.

McCloud was spreading the noose, fondling his hangman's knot with loving care. He had a black cap tucked in his belt and when Frank came up to him he pulled it out.

Frank Taylor's young face was beginning to show a trace of worry. His eyes grew restless as they searched the face-paved expanse on all sides.

"You won't find him," said McCloud in a whisper. "I took care of that."

Frank faced him, suddenly white with anger. "You've murdered him!"

McCloud went into action. He tried to slip the black cap over Frank's head but he could not. Three guards leaped up the steps to hold Frank in firm grips. The cap was pulled down in place. Roughly they shoved Frank to the trapdoor and then McCloud, with help, slid the noose over his head and drew it tight.

"Ladies and gentlemen," said McCloud with pious intonation. "I hope this'll be a lesson to you. This's the fate of evildoers in Pioneer. We ain't had no justice here in a long time, but by God we've got it now! This gent tried to grab all the cows and all the gold in sight and so we ain't got no use for such an unrespectable citizen in a respectable town and here and now we are about to terminate his youth after a fair and legal trial durin' which he was proved guilty as hell of all them things that's been happenin'. The law has tooken its course. Amen. Boys, the . . ."

There came a shriek from the outskirts of the crowd and then a mad rush away from the east end of the street. Suddenly the cry spread with the wings of terror and men leaped hastily for cover.

Fifty longhorns, horn rattling on horn, hurtled toward the gallows, excited by the yells about them but terrified by the shrieking fiend behind them who slashed them with a quirt and made a whirlwind with a serape.

"Yee-yip-yipyip-yippi YI!" yelled Lynn.

And the crowd fled before the approaching wall of beef. They were afoot and the consequences of that fact swept away all reason. Long before the front rank of the herd touched the gallows, all spectators had vanished and could be seen clinging precariously to roofs and false-fronts on either side of the square while others peered from doorways, ready to bolt again.

Isolated on the gallows were McCloud, three guards and their victim.

McCloud instantly thought of fight as the steers rumbled by on either side. He grabbed his Colt and started to snap down on the rider made phantom by the billowing dust. A shot drove the steers even faster, but it had come from their wake. McCloud's gun, with a bright gash in the stock, flipped to the platform and McCloud was holding his wrist.

The three guards felt needlessly exposed, not sure but what the next shot would down any one of them, uncertain that the gallows was safe from the steers who shook it to its foundation in their passage.

Enwrapped in the dust now, the guards took the wiser course and threw up their hands.

With drawn guns, Lynn charged up the steps on the buckskin. He leaned out of the saddle and took the rope from around Frank's neck and slashed the bonds which confined the boy's arms. Frank yanked off his black hood and grabbed up McCloud's fallen gun.

"Stay where you are!" warned Lynn. And with Frank up behind him he rode down the steps and up the front of the general store. Men went out the back door when the two came in the front.

Presently all was quiet in Pioneer and the steers, no longer driven, quietly searched out the grass on the plain beyond. Two by two and ten by ten, cattlemen ventured forth into the street. The guards, not certain but what they were still covered from the general store, stood with their hands stiffly in the air, still shocked by the fact that a man marked dead had turned up so astonishingly. McCloud still sat on the planking and nursed his hand.

A clear voice from the store struck into the throng. Lynn, both guns showing above a molasses barrel, sang out, "Gents, you've made a mistake. And I ain't clearin' out of this town until you fix it up."

McCloud found courage. He stood up and waved his arm in a sweeping motion. "Go get him!"

"The first man up here gets it," said Lynn. And behind another barrel inside the door, Frank's gun was also showing and his eyes looked eager to see a target down its sights after his late injustices.

"I got the evidence," said Lynn, "that Fanner McCloud has played you gents for suckers." The crowd stiffened and

Lynn surged on. "He pulled all them robberies himself and then tried to cover them up by hangin' Frank Taylor and incidentally getting Frank's spread. Gents, if you care to look, I'll lay you ten to one that you'll find last night's dispatch box under McCloud's floor. Go look and see."

Several went and looked. McCloud started to find a way through the crowd.

A short time later, the searchers charged forth with a yell. "There's eight dispatch boxes under that floor! Don't let that guy get away!"

McCloud had stopped moving. He had a gun jammed into his stomach and behind the gun stood ex-Sheriff Hawkins.

"There's your murderer! There's your thief!" shouted Lynn. "And there's the gallows!"

About midnight the celebration of the hanging of Fanner McCloud began to wane and Frank and Lynn withdrew to the stable and saddled up.

Hawkins met them as they led their horses forth.

"Lynn," said Hawkins, "I got to thank you." And he gave his star a burnishing brush. "I hope you'll stick around this country for a while. I allus did like you Texans. But how the hell did you know where them dispatch boxes was?"

"Yeah," said Lynn, swinging up, "that is a puzzle, ain't it. C'mon, Frank. I never did get a chance to look at this ranch of yours."

# Ride 'Em, Cowboy!

# CHAPTER ONE

# The Winner

THE Ellensburg Rodeo was in full tide.

Twenty-five thousand packed the stands and made a blurred sea surging up from the other side of the track.

The arena boss and the judges and wranglers were hurrying on important errands across the wet green turf of the arena.

Flags and Indians and violent-shirted punchers made the day loud and bright.

The band was playing "Cheyenne, Cheyenne," but Long Tom Branner, sitting on the gate of chute five, saw and heard very little of it. He was watching with hungry eyes Miss Vicky Stuart as she climbed up to the runway and came toward the chute which held Dynamite.

Long Tom sighed. Vicky was all in white, all creamy silk and leather. And just now she was pushing a strand of corn-colored hair back under her Stetson. Her golden spurs clink-jingled and they made the only sound in the world which Long Tom Branner could hear.

He hooked his high heels more solidly into the third bar and sat up straighter, prepared for the worst.

"Give him hell, Vicky," said Long Tom.

She stopped and looked across at him. Dynamite was screaming murder and death and kicking the chute into splinters.

"Thank you, I will."

He wished she wouldn't treat him so. She wasn't this rough on the rest of the world. To everybody else she was a charming kid with more nerve and skill than most buckaroos possess.

He knew that if he said anything he would make it worse. But suddenly he heard himself saying, "Watch him. I had him last year at Pendleton and he sunfishes right after he takes his first jump. I—"

"Thank you," said Vicky with so much sweetness that it was acid. "I am sure it is very kind of the champion bronco buster of the world to give me advice."

Long Tom felt his face getting red and knew he would get mad in a minute. Damn it, why couldn't she treat him like she used to when Old Man Stuart paid him wages?

A devil prodded him. She looked so cool and self-possessed there on the runway.

"Yeah," said Branner. "It ain't everybody that needs it."

She lifted her head and then abruptly whirled and swung down into the chute.

Another devil jabbed Long Tom. "Don't fall off. You'll get mud on yourself!"

She didn't even look at him. Settling her hat, she stood with feet wide apart on the rails and Dynamite lunged and screamed under her while two punchers tried to hold his head quiet.

"Drop!" yelled the man at the gate.

Vicky dropped into the saddle. The brute lunged sideways and almost caught her leg.

"Let 'im go!" she yelled.

The gate swung wide and the blind came off and Dynamite went plunging like a rocket into the open.

Long Tom held his breath. The arena was muddy and Dynamite never bucked straight up. He sunfished.

Off was Vicky's white hat. She beat it against the bellowing demon's flanks. She dug deep with her golden spurs and Dynamite went five feet off the ground. He sunfished, head lowered, fighting the hackamore and when he hit he was stiff-legged.

Vicky took the shock. She beat harder with her hat and dug deeper with her spurs and above the band and the crowd and the announcer could be heard her cry, "Go it, you black devil!"

Long Tom was still holding his breath as he counted. Dynamite was exploding all over the sky. Vicky was limp-shouldered, as graceful as a gull.

"Go it, you black devil!"

Dynamite slipped as he hit, fell heavily on his side and leaped furiously up again.

Vicky whipped his flank with her white hat and dug her golden spurs.

"Go it!"

The gun cracked and she had made a ride. Two mounted men swerved in beside her, one to grab Dynamite's head and the other to haul Vicky from the still-lunging mount. She made it and Dynamite was headed away, still fighting.

The rider lowered her to the ground and she ran with swift, excited steps back to the chutes.

*Dynamite was exploding all over the sky. Vicky was limp-shouldered, as graceful as a gull.*

She passed within three feet of Long Tom but she didn't even look up at him when he said, "Swell ride, Vicky."

Gloomily he looked at the grandstand again. Everybody was cheering, but that didn't matter. Everybody was going crazy about that ride, and that was natural.

Vicky Stuart was the enigma of the buckaroos. She was slightly built and had the manners of a duchess and talked much better English. She was the kind of girl, on appearance, that one would expect to haunt teas and operas, but, marvel of marvels, she could take a beating on the back of a bucking horse and always come off smiling, just as though she had done nothing so very unusual.

Long Tom sighed.

For two years, ever since Old Man Stuart had died, Long Tom Branner had tried to keep near Vicky. At least a dozen times he had striven to make a serious proposal, but Vicky was as quick afoot as she was mounted. She always slid out.

Long Tom knew, vaguely, what was wrong. There was nothing too terrible about his personal appearance, as he was lean and young. But for some reason unknown to himself he kept winning championships as a rider. And the more he won, the colder Vicky Stuart got.

A long time ago, when he was just a puncher riding for her old man, he and Vicky had almost reached an understanding. Long Tom had not pushed his suit, thinking that if he could make a name, he would be worthy of her hand.

And then Stuart had died, leaving nothing. And Vicky, raised among horsemen and an excellent rider in her own right, had suddenly taken it into her head to win the world for her own.

There is no one quite so alone as a famous bronc twister. And with Vicky high-hatting him, Long Tom could not help but feel low.

He had to do something.

He had to somehow make Vicky understand that he loved her and wanted her. . . .

"Mr. Branner," said the arena boss respectfully, riding close, "you're out on Jesse James from chute six in about a minute."

"Yeah," said Long Tom. "Yeah, that's right. I forgot."

He climbed up to the walk and went to the top of the next chute.

Jesse James was a sorrel with one blue eye and one brown eye. He had feet like ashcans and was so thickly built that he could throw most men in the first three leaps.

The band changed off to "Tipperary."

Long Tom stood up on the rails and watched Jesse James lunge against the bars. Tom's feet were wide apart and suddenly he could concentrate on only one thing, this ride.

The announcer roared, "Long Tom Branner! The Champeeen bronco buster of the world! Coming out of chute six!"

Everything hushed. The band stopped and the judges were motionless and the crowd forgot peanuts and sat very still.

Jesse James lashed out with a savage kick and splintered the gate.

"Let 'er go!" said Long Tom.

He dropped, jamming toes into stirrups. He heard the

gate whine as it was rushed back. It was suddenly light in the chute.

Jesse James drew in like a spring compressing. Suddenly he streaked straight out and up. Ten feet from the chute his hind feet hit.

Long Tom fanned and roweled.

Jesse James went skyward, turning. Earth and sun and people and band were all scrambled in a swift montage. Jar, slam, blowie! With buckjumps vicious enough to kill a man, the outlaw fought his rider.

Sunfish, lunge and then swap ends!

Indians and punchers and judges and wet earth all mixed up with clouds.

Long Tom rode straight up, head high, a grin on his lips, shoulders loose, hat swinging in rhythm to the leaps of the maniac horse.

In a moment the gun would go. And nothing Jesse James could do could disturb this lean and graceful rider.

And in that instant a horrible thought hit Long Tom. If he made this ride, he would be beating Vicky. She was the runner-up. He would not lose his belt as it was not at stake. He did not need the purse. And if he beat Vicky Stuart, he would never have a chance. Not a chance.

He swung his arm around and touched his horn.

And the gun banged.

He felt funny. That was the first time he had ever done that. He had pulled leather!

A pair of riders jerked the horse one way and Long Tom the other. Long Tom eased himself down to the ground.

Vaguely he could hear people cheering and the announcer was bellowing something which was flattering, and a rider said, "Gee, that was pretty, Mr. Branner."

Long Tom went swinging back to the chutes. He was irritated suddenly by that "Mr. Branner." Everybody called him "Mr. Branner" now and nobody ever came near him. It was as though he had measles or something.

Before he got to the chutes he saw Vicky. Three mounted judges were gathered about her and she was slim and straight and angry.

When Long Tom came near they all turned and stared at him, so he edged in that direction.

He could see that Vicky was mad. When she got mad she got taller and prettier and her eyes were hot sparks. She got very dignified and held her chin high and frost was white upon her words.

"Mr. Branner," said a judge, "we saw you touch your horn. Possibly we were mistaken. You were making a beautiful ride and I can't understand. What was the cause of it?"

"I touched it," said Long Tom.

"Of course, you know that that will give today to Miss Stuart," said the judge.

"Yes," said Long Tom.

Vicky looked at him levelly. Her clenched hand was trembling at her side. "You deliberately threw that contest to me!"

Long Tom looked uneasy. He could not quite understand this. What was there about winning which could make her so mad?

"You're despicable," said Vicky coldly.

"Huh?" said Long Tom.

"You purposely threw this contest to humiliate me!"

Long Tom blinked and then suddenly he was angry. He stared at her with narrowed eyes. "Well, why not?" he said savagely. "There's no percentage in beating a woman!"

He turned on his heel and stalked away.

CHAPTER TWO

# Vicky Retaliates

VICKY STUART walked through the Indian village which was studded with horses and papooses on this, the second day of the rodeo. Here and there sat heavy-jowled elders upon blankets, looking very wise and self-satisfied. In the tepees and back of them scurried the women, dressed in beaded elkskin but working just the same.

A few young bucks wearing business suits and braids looked cautiously at Vicky as she passed. They knew her and were most respectful. The old men nodded and the women smiled brightly and the papooses gurgled.

But Vicky's mood was black. Her silk-crowned head was held high and the golden spurs jangled viciously as she stamped over the green turf.

A hundred dollars was heavy in the pocket of her batwings. The hundred-dollar day money which she had won by Long Tom's condemned dishonesty. Nothing had ever been as heavy as those paper bills. She could feel them dragging down her spirit as though she were burdened with anvils.

She had to stop to let a young kid get a string of mustangs in line and she looked around her and had the funny feeling that the whole Indian village was about to leap at her.

A young buck was arguing vigorously with a squaw, evidently

his mother, and the woman was shaking her head. Vicky knew the boy as a good bulldogger.

She saw them stop and look at her and nod. She forced herself to say, "Hello, Bucking Colt. How's everything?"

"Rotten," said the youth, spitting. "I've got the fastest pony here and she won't let me have a nickel to bet on him."

Vicky straightened up. She gave her Stetson a swift tug and stepped nearer to Bucking Colt. Out of her batwing pocket she pulled the hundred dollars and extended it.

He took it swiftly enough.

His mother tried to stop him. "He spendum, get drunk!"

"Throw it away for all I care," said Vicky.

She went on. But she didn't feel right yet. Before twenty-five thousand people, Long Tom had pulled leather and now he was going around telling everybody that "there's no percentage in beating a woman!"

She looked coolly beautiful. But she felt mean and little inside.

This had started so long ago that she had almost forgotten the beginning. Long Tom had been a bashful, gangling kid, getting thirty a month for helping handle Stuart's rodeo string. Nobody had thought he would ever amount to much because he was so quiet. But he had begun to practice riding and roping. He had worked and he had grown.

And if he had not persisted in showing her how he did everything, she would never have gotten so mad at him. He was always so superior, always telling her what to do and what not to do, always bossing her around.

She had said that she would show him someday. And when Stuart had died, leaving her without a cent but with a riding education seldom equaled, she had started on her way.

Long Tom had a belt. A beautiful belt. He wore it all the time. It was diamond-studded and upon it were letters in gold, "World's Champion Buckeroo." That was hateful. She could never get such a belt. She was a woman. They always told her how surprised they were that she could ride, damn them! Punchers were always making up to her with, "You're too pretty to wear chaps."

Damn them!

She hated men. She hated punchers. But most of all she hated Long Tom Branner.

He was so sure of himself, so superior! He knew he was lean and good-looking. He knew that women fell all over themselves to get at him. He knew that he looked like a god on the back of a raging horse.

Tan Stetson and golden, glittering belt.

She hated him!

She got to the gate and the ticket-taker stood back to tip his hat and let her through. She went swinging through the carnival grounds and the hoot-hoot bing-bang of the merry-go-round infuriated her.

She kicked at a tin can and sent it soaring.

The contests were still going on. Today she had a good horse. A good, tough horse. Whiskers, they called him. He sometimes went straight up and came down on his side. She'd teach him manners.

As she came through the grandstand side, people turned and looked at her, the men very admiringly. Somebody made so bold as to say, "Lo, Vicky." She froze him into a pillar of ice.

She realized that she was doing things backwards. She should have walked around to the other gate in the first place. But she had been too angry to obey anything.

Down below her she saw groups of mounts on the track just under the stands and knew that the pony express race was about to begin.

Something was happening. A youngster was standing on one foot and holding his side and arguing with the arena boss down on the turf. Suddenly she knew what was wrong. The youngster was part of this pony express race and he had been hurt in the bucking contest of the day.

Suddenly she was blinded by a glitter and she whirled to see Long Tom with belt aglitter just under the railing not twenty feet from her. So he was going to be in this race!

Determinedly she slid through the railing and ran to the side of the youngster. She said swiftly, "I'll take your place. The prize money don't matter. I'll pay it win or lose."

Before they could answer she was halfway back to the boy's three mounts.

Long Tom looked at her, startled. She turned away and inspected the saddle a puncher held out to her.

The race was a relay of horses in which the rider had to change his own saddle. Three mounts and three times around the track.

The starter saw that all was ready and held up his gun.

It banged and the five contestants began hastily to saddle. Vicky had more reason to win than any of them. She was the first away. Flirting mud from the mount's flying hoofs, she spurted past Long Tom without even a glance.

She plied her quirt and the track raced by and when she passed back of the chutes and bandstand, the band was making hash out of the "Light Cavalry Overture."

The fence blurred as she came around the turn into the stretch. Ahead she saw that the puncher had her horse out. She was half a dozen lengths ahead.

Mount still running, she flung herself off and skidded him to a stop. She flipped up the saddle skirt and unfastened the cinch buckle and flung the saddle to the other mount. She bothered not about the cinch this time.

Quirt flailing, she rocketed off just as Long Tom plunged up to his second mount.

This time the band was making better time, she noted. The sousaphone was the only one behind.

The fence blurred and the stands blurred and again off came her saddle. Looking across it when she got it on the third mount, she saw Long Tom leading all the rest but at least half the track behind her.

Her grin was deadly.

Very carefully she fastened the cinch. She took a handkerchief and dusted the saddle. In a leisurely fashion she mounted. Long Tom was streaking up. He came off his mount to change saddles in a blur of activity. The others were stringing in.

Vicky started out at a canter as though only to enjoy the scenery. Long Tom rocketed past her on the run. Vicky kept her horse down to a steady trot.

The band, she noted as she passed, was all behind the sousaphone this time.

Long Tom was in seconds before she leisurely cantered up. The others thundered across the line just behind her.

Long Tom sat his lathered horse, breathing hard and staring at her.

She was not at all concerned.

The arena boss came over to them on the run and the stands craned their necks to see this that was happening under their noses.

"What was wrong?" said the arena boss indignantly to Vicky.

She flipped up her hat brim and stared coolly at Long Tom. Then she shrugged and turned to the arena boss.

"There's no percentage in beating a conceited fool."

CHAPTER THREE

# Last Event

IT was the third and last day of the rodeo. All morning it
had rained and the track was soggy and the turf was like
grease. But during the early part of the contest there had only
been clouds and now the sun was threatening to break through.

The rodeo was drawing to a close and the last contest
rides were done. Two punchers were in the hospital with
cracked bones and another was not feeling too well, though
he hobbled around. The slippery grass was murderous. A
bulldogger's heels could find no hold and just kept plowing.
Broncs went down at unexpected moments.

Only the trick riders had come through unscathed, though
wet ropes had not been easy to handle.

Tension had come into the day with dawn for Long Tom
Branner. And with the rain it had increased. Vicky had not
come through on the bucking contest but Long Tom had.
His mount, Crabapple, had fallen three times in three jumps
and he had been shaken up more than he cared to admit.

But his belt still glittered and people still persisted in calling
him that distant, if respectful, "Mr. Branner."

He was uneasy when he saw anyone laughing from afar.
He knew there was a great deal of merriment in the air about
what Vicky had done.

But she was not cocky about it. She merely continued to avoid him, which was just as bad.

And so he sat on the top of a chute gate and hooked in his heels and stared gloomily across at the stands.

It was funny. Here he had worked like a fool to get to be a champion. He had ridden buckers in his dreams and in his waking hours for six years. And he was the champion and everybody called him "Mr. Branner."

He had started out just to be able to hand the world to the girl he loved. And she hated him for it.

A long, long time ago he had tried to convince her that he wasn't just a bashful kid. He had almost broken his neck more than once to show her how he could ride.

And before that things had not been too bad. She had been as nice to him as she was to anybody else. She used to like to steal a couple of Stuart's horses after the day's show and go ride out with him when the moon made everything blue.

But somehow he had never had the courage to press that suit. He had made those dozen stumbling, blushing efforts and each time he had failed miserably. And so he had gone out and conquered the highest throne in the rodeo world just to be able to get high enough to make her see him.

Yes, he had come near breaking his neck for a girl and now when she talked to him at all, she bit him.

But she wasn't like that to the rest of the world. She was all smiles and kindness and men respected her as a beautiful woman and an excellent rider.

Why the devil had she ever taken up this riding anyhow?

he asked himself. She had no reason like he had to go around smashing herself up on tricky man-killers. Somehow it wasn't ladylike.

Suddenly he straightened up. There was Vicky, walking down the fence toward the chutes from the back gate. One glimpse of her was all it took to make his bitterness fade. There was a patch of sunlight hurrying across the arena and it struck Vicky and her golden spurs glowed and the silver concha of her chin thong glittered.

He wished he could always see her that way.

Unfortunately for Long Tom, the diamonds and gold in his championship belt threw out blinding sparks in the same flash of sunlight. Vicky swerved her course toward him.

Over to Long Tom's right, half a dozen riders were hazing twenty horses into line, getting ready for the last event, the wild horse race. The din of yips and quirts and snorts and hoofs was deafening but Long Tom did not even hear them. He was watching Vicky come near.

She nodded to the arena boss as he trotted by and the arena boss smiled and tipped his hat.

Long Tom uncomfortably realized that she was going to approach him personally and talk to him. He slid down off the gate and stood in an attitude which looked defiant but which was merely defensive.

He was a pretty picture of a puncher standing there, but he didn't know it. He was something which had just stepped down from the rodeo posters.

And Vicky did not miss the attitude.

"Two men," said Vicky, "were laid out this afternoon."

"Yeah," said Long Tom.

"And that will leave their places in the wild horse race."

Long Tom looked at her suspiciously.

"And," said Vicky, "there isn't any objection to you and I taking those places."

"So what?" said Long Tom.

Vicky was very casual. She flicked her quirt against one flaring white wing of her chaps and looked at Long Tom's glittering belt.

"There are two mankillers in that crowd," said Vicky, indicating the herd of wild horses which was still coming out. "Some of the boys are betting that neither one of them can even be saddled out in the arena."

"Yeah?" said Long Tom.

Vicky smiled, but not very pleasantly. "Yeah. We've never tried this. We've never matched ourselves up in open contest on broncs. One of those horses is Thunder and the other is Wild Bill. We obey the rules. We saddle and then go once around the track, if we can."

"And?" said Long Tom.

"And I've got three thousand dollars saved up, Long Tom Branner."

"So have I."

"Okay, Mr. Champion Bronc Twisteroo, put up or shut up. If I win I get three thousand cash and you never say another word to me about anything such as how to ride. And if you win . . ."

Long Tom didn't know how he had suddenly gotten so

bold. He squared off. "If I win, you don't have to pay up. You marry me."

She gasped and stood motionless.

"That's right," said Long Tom swiftly. "You think you're better than me. Okay, you've got a chance to prove it."

She was breathless with shock. "But I didn't think . . . I mean that's . . ."

"Put up or shut up!" said Long Tom truculently. "You win and you'll never be bothered by me again and you'll be richer by three thousand dollars. I win and I win. Is that clear?"

She colored and raised her head defiantly. "Yes, that's clear. God, but you hate yourself!"

"Yeah?" said Long Tom.

"I know what would happen to me if I lost!" said Vicky.

"I doubt that you'd keep the bargain," snapped Long Tom.

That was the blow which ignited the powder magazine of her anger. She got white and then whirled and stamped away.

Long Tom watched her go. He didn't feel just right. He didn't want her to fight Thunder or Wild Bill around that slippery, mucky track.

But she hated him when he refused to beat her.

And this time he would beat her!

"Joe!" yelled Long Tom to a rider. "I'm taking Bart Johnson's place on Wild Bill."

The puncher looked startled. "Yes, Mr. Branner." He turned in his saddle. "Hey, run Wild Bill back in!"

Long Tom strode across the soft turf toward the stands. The arena boss had stopped beside Vicky and now he quirted up and came trotting toward Long Tom.

"Miss Stuart is riding Thunder," said the arena boss in a surprised tone of voice.

"I'm on Wild Bill," said the twister.

"For God's sake!" said the arena boss, hurrying away.

Bart Johnson's two friends were hurrying across with saddle and hackamore to Long Tom. And the friends of the other injured man were loping toward Vicky. Everywhere men were running with saddles or harassing snorting, stamping mustangs into various places in the arena.

The announcer blared through the speakers, "Laaadies and genulmen, there are two additions, two startling additions, to the wild horse race! The last event on the program and the last event of the rodeo. The young lady in white whom you have seeeen taking events for three days against all comers, one of the world's greatest riders, Miss Vicky Stuart!"

A roar of sound swept through the stands. More than one gentleman up there had lost his heart during the last three days, though Vicky might be a dozen worlds away from them and would never even know their names, much less ever see them.

The announcer went on. "And over there to your right is a tall young fellow with hair pants and tan Stetson. He looks pretty gaudy around the middle. That glitter you see is a belt studded with diamonds and worked with gold and on it is written, 'World's Champion Buckeroo.' Ladies and genulmen, Mr. Long Tom Branner!"

There was another roar and Long Tom blushed and got busy with the saddle.

Wild Bill was forced up. He had his ears laid back and his eyes were wilder than his name. His nostrils were flaring and he tried to strike out with his front feet. A puncher tried to hold his head down but was sometimes lifted clear off the earth.

The other puncher finally got hold on the head and began to bite Wild Bill's ear to distract his attention.

Vicky's Thunder was striking out with vicious hoofs and screaming vengeance while her two punchers fought to make him stand still.

All over the arena men were fighting twenty broncs in separate groups and more than one shin was being scarred. Punchers were fighting and swearing and horses were fighting and swearing.

At last all was at least as calm as the Battle of the Marne. Saddle, mount, ride and the first one to make a complete circuit of the track was the winner.

Vicky looked across the surging field at Long Tom. Her jaw was set and she blazed with determination. Once and for all she would show him.

And Long Tom also blazed. Here was the chance he had prayed for and no punches would be pulled this time.

A gun banged. Twenty mounts were startled into furious activity by the unaccustomed slap of saddles on their backs. Mounts and men went down in mad, muddy fights.

Long Tom's helpers threw the saddle on Wild Bill and the old bronc had never shown such deadly fury. Wrenching a tormentor clear of the earth, Wild Bill tried to plunge away. He was held down by sheer strength.

Hurriedly Long Tom reached under for the cinch and brought it back. As he fastened it, Wild Bill surged away from him.

Vicky had her saddle in place but Thunder was not going to let any more weight be put upon him. She thrust her foot into the stirrup and tried to swing up, holding the reins so that Thunder had to curve in toward her. But Thunder exploded.

Wild Bill reared and struck down, missing. A puncher got the blind back on him and for an instant the outlaw stood still in fright.

Long Tom leaped into the saddle. But before he could find the other stirrup, Wild Bill began to explode.

The flapping stirrup banged into Long Tom's shin. He kicked at it, on his way to the zenith. He found it when Wild Bill came down stiff-legged and roaring with rage.

Wild Bill was not to be beaten so easily. He began to buckjump, short vicious stabs at earth with straight hoofs. He sailed upward again and came down the other way around.

Long Tom rode and rode gracefully. But it was one thing to stick and quite another to get this screaming half ton of fighting horse headed out for the track.

Vicky had no eyes for anything but the saddle. Thunder was going round and round as she strove to mount.

Abruptly she reversed the tug on the reins and, for an instant, the mount was still. She sprang up. Thunder leaped skyward. Holding with her knees alone, she got the other stirrup. And then the grandstand was mixed up with the chutes and the fence was vertical and nineteen other horses were bucking through the clouds.

52

Thunder wanted to run but he was headed wrong. She tried to turn him and he fought for his head, lunging blindly through scattering groups of men and horses.

Mud and flying batwings made up the world for an instant and then Vicky saw that she was going right. She saw something else. The flash of diamonds in a belt told her that Long Tom was the first to reach the track and start around.

With a mad rush, Thunder plowed through the white rails of the track, sending splinters flying. He almost fell as he skidded in the mud. Vicky pulled him upright by yanking the reins.

Long Tom was on the track. But Wild Bill started into another fury of bucking and Tom was too much of a buckaroo not to fan.

Wild Bill tried to rush the wrong way around and Long Tom harassed him into turning in another direction. Out of half an eye, Long Tom saw the white blur on an exploding mount and knew that he and Vicky were the first ones out in the track. It was treacherous work here, as any moment a mount might fall.

"Ride 'em, Vicky!" yelled Long Tom from sheer exuberance.

Suddenly he saw her just beside him, headed in the right direction, quirting Thunder.

"Go it, you devil!" cried Vicky.

A panic hit both horses in the same instant. Like catapulted arrows they shot forward. Long Tom was ahead half a length and the glitter of his belt was in Vicky's eyes.

The grandstand fled. Thunder tried to lunge through the board fence but she swerved him back. She hit against Wild

Bill and both mounts abruptly broke into a mad fury of bucking.

Wild Bill was lunging and buckjumping as he went ahead. But Thunder sunfished with unexpected vigor.

She was half unseated by the collision as she had had to withdraw a leg. And now she could not get the stirrup back.

Thunder hit earth at an angle and started to fall. Vicky braced herself for a jump free. But Thunder suddenly recovered and lunged sideways in the opposite direction.

The skid and reversal were so sudden that Vicky's grip broke on the reins and suddenly she no longer had her saddle. She was falling to the left.

Desperately in that moment she strove to free her left foot from the stirrup. But it was twisted and the golden spur was caught.

She hit earth on her shoulder and it would have been broken had the mud not been so soft.

Above her she could see a lunging saddle against the sky and a foot from her face struck the hoofs of Thunder.

The sudden release of weight made the mustang leap ahead. Wild Bill also leaped ahead.

But not until that instant did Long Tom Branner know that Vicky was off with one foot hung, and would be either dragged to death by her insane mount, or mangled when Thunder went through the fence.

Immediately there was nothing which could be done. Wild Bill was in full stride, a length ahead of Thunder.

And then Long Tom did a strange thing.

He yanked Wild Bill to the left with such strength that the outlaw was broadsided to the track.

A matter of feet from Long Tom's shoulder and leg, Thunder was coming blind.

And Long Tom jerked his mount's head to the right and up and pulled with all his might, leaning back.

Unbalanced twice on a slippery track, only one thing could happen.

Wild Bill went down. Went down to throw Long Tom Branner under the striking hoofs of another maniac horse.

Vicky had not been dragged twenty feet, so swiftly had it happened. Wild Bill piled Thunder up and the two mounts went down, entangled and screaming.

But Long Tom had not misgauged. Before he hit the track himself, despite the stunning blows upon his shoulders, he had seized the stirrup which held Vicky's foot and his own weight ripped it free.

With a loud thud, Long Tom hit.

Wild Bill and Thunder struggled up and suddenly began to run.

From afar came the wranglers to help. The grandstand was so still that hoofbeats were very loud.

Long Tom turned over in the mud. Vicky pushed herself to a sitting position and wiped a daub from her right eye.

Long Tom did not even feel his bruises. He went toward her on his hands and knees. "Are you all right?" he said hoarsely.

"I . . . I was sc-c-c-cared you'd be killed!" wailed Vicky unexpectedly.

55

"I'm all right," said Long Tom. "Gosh, I was scared stiff myself."

And then a very strange thing happened. Vicky, sitting in the mud beside him, looked intently into his face. He had lost. They both had lost. And he had thought so much of her that he had risked being brained. . . .

Suddenly she grabbed his arms and buried her face in his shoulder. "Please," she wept. "Please forgive me, Long Tom. I . . . I've acted like a fool! I won't fight with you any more!"

He wrapped his arms about her and implanted a muddy kiss upon her brow.

Suddenly he began to grin. "The hell you won't. But what the devil? I'd rather fight with you across the breakfast table than across a chute gate."

"Oh, Long Tom."

And neither one of them heard the cheers which came from twenty-five thousand throats.

*Vicky and Long Tom*

# Boss of the Lazy B

# Chapter One

SOMETIME before dawn the posse had surrounded the shack and now with the horizon streaking with gray they lay on their stomachs in the tall grass, chilled by the desert wind but hot for battle.

Big Bill Bailey was hunched down on the sheriff's right, taking the most advantageous position because he owned the biggest spread in the Rio Carlos country. Big Bill lived up to his name. He rode a veritable mammoth of a roan and his hats were gigantic—they had to be. He stood six feet six and his weight matched his size.

With a John B. for a crown and a quirt for a scepter, Big Bill ruled the Lazy B, which covered more territory than the Kingdom of Jfradersweganstan.

But of late his ten thousand beefy subjects had been mysteriously missing their mothers and brothers and had developed a unique habit of giving birth to strangely branded calves. Fighting sheep was bad enough without fighting rustlers as well, but Big Bill never got ruffled about such things. He had little to say and usually what he did say was delivered after prolonged thought. In this case he had mentioned that it might be a good idea to track down a stolen band, so Con Mathews of the Flying M and the rest of the nearby ranchers had collected the sheriff and had taken the trail.

And now they knew that the probable owner of that trail, one Spick Murphy, was in this mountain shack peacefully dreaming of his plunder.

Or maybe he was watching with a cocked rifle.

It was all the same to the posse. Spick Murphy was already as good as hanged for the murdering half-breed he was.

He was of very unsavory reputation, Spick Murphy. His father was an Irishman and his mother an Apache squaw and between the two they had bequeathed upon him both a countenance angelic and a soul diabolic. He oscillated between the two extremes, given to voluntary acts of kindness one moment and shooting a man in the back the next. Uncertain, unpredictable, hated and liked at one and the same time, he had often styled himself the Robin Hood of Rio Carlos, but it is doubtful if Robin Hood had killed sixteen men at the age of twenty.

The sun started on its climb to the zenith and the posse still waited patiently. Sooner or later Spick would have to come out and get some water at the spring which bubbled a hundred yards from the door, and when he did, things would begin to happen.

One of Big Bill's chief talents was the ability to wait. For three years he had patiently waited for Susan Price to say the word which would make her Mrs. Bailey. He did not push the matter because Susan was not that kind of a girl. She was not interested in his money as her father, Sam Price, the ultra-famous criminal lawyer, could have bought and sold Bailey twice. And so Bailey had waited, always present, always reliable, always dependable, just as he was waiting now for Spick Murphy to come out.

Some of the posse began to mumble as the sun scorched their backs. Sheriff Doyle mopped his huge red face and squirmed.

"Hell, I'd rather rush the place than stay here and broil," complained stringy Con Mathews.

"What about it, Big Bill?" said Sheriff Doyle.

Big Bill was silent for two or three minutes before he answered. "He'll have to come out sooner or later. If not today, tomorrow."

"Y'mean y'think we'll wait *that* long?" demanded Con Mathews.

After a while, Big Bill said, "If your cattle aren't worth that much to you, it's your decision."

"All right. I was just askin', that's all," replied Con. "When he comes out I'll drill him and then we can go home."

"No sir," said Sheriff Doyle. "I got to go through an election in a couple months. This trial will be fine for me. Don't you plug him."

"All right," agreed Con irritably. "Let's all go down and play patty-cake with him."

Big Bill was silent for a long time and then he said, "When he comes out, let him go to the spring. When he gets there, open up on the door and yell for him to surrender."

"Okay, Big Bill," said Sheriff Doyle.

"There must be another with him," argued Con. "What'll we do with *him*?"

Big Bill thought that over. "We'll wait and see what happens."

The sun climbed higher and higher and Big Bill's big repeater watch bing-binged ten o'clock in his pocket. As though that were the signal, the cabin door swung open and a dumpy individual known as "Cheyenne" Shorty came out swinging a pail. He went to the spring, stopped and filled his bucket. After throwing some cold water on his face he turned around and started back for the door.

Sheriff Doyle bellowed, "Stick 'em up!"

Cheyenne Shorty whirled toward the sound. He dropped the bucket and the water splashed over his boots. Smoke barked from his right hand and Doyle's hat sailed like a swallow.

The crash of rifles was ragged but effective. Cheyenne Shorty dropped with a clatter over the water bucket and lay still.

"You there in the cabin!" roared Doyle. "Come out with your hands grabbin' sky."

Spick Murphy's jeering voice called, "And get killed?"

"We won't shoot if you come peaceable," shouted Doyle.

"I wouldn't trust you with a coyote's dinner," yelled Spick. "Send somebody down for protection and I'll come."

Big Bill thought it over and then stood up. "I'll go down."

Doyle grabbed at his boots. "Don't! That's just one of his tricks."

"He knows you'll kill him if he tries anything," said Big Bill. "Hey, you down there. I'm coming."

The posse held their collective breaths. Big Bill sauntered down the slope toward the cabin as though out to admire the wildflowers instead of pushing them up.

He went leisurely enough, a lumbering colossus with an impassive face. He was not carrying his rifle and he had not drawn the gun at his hip.

"The fool," said Con.

"He's either awful dumb or awful brave," said a puncher in the rear.

"If he didn't go, we'd camp here for a month," retorted Doyle.

Big Bill walked slowly up to the cabin door which was still open. "Come on out, Spick."

The interior was dim and silent.

Big Bill stepped inside. He sensed movement above him and ducked. A table leg hit a glancing blow on his shoulders. Big Bill struck the floor, rolling and drawing at the same time.

Spick's head was silhouetted against the window for an instant and Big Bill fired.

Spick dropped, and the table leg rolled up to Big Bill's boot and stopped. For a full minute nothing else happened and then Big Bill got up and looked at Spick.

The bandit's head was creased as Big Bill had intended and everything was as it should be.

Big Bill stepped to the door and called out, "All right."

The posse came down the hill on the run.

"What was the sense of his doin' that?" said the perspiring Doyle.

"Nervy gent," said Con. "He didn't have a gun to his name and that was his way of gettin' one. See? Cheyenne had the only six-shooter in the place."

"All right," said Big Bill. "Let's get him to town."

# Chapter Two

SUSAN PRICE was taking her afternoon ride alone, wondering a little why Big Bill Bailey had not appeared on the scene that morning. She was not so very concerned about it as she knew he would have an excellent excuse.

That was one of the main troubles with Big Bill Bailey. He was as reliable as the huge repeating watch he carried—and at times dependability can be carried a little too far. He never surprised Susan with anything. Guitars and midnight serenades were as much out of his line as were waist-deep bows and flattery. In fact, Big Bill was likely to be somewhat tongue-tied among the ladies, holding them in a reverence which was flattering only for a short time.

But everybody in the Rio Carlos country knew that Big Bill Bailey and Susan Price would someday be married. It was the natural thing and the only men who growled about it were rejected suitors who claimed it must be Big Bill's money—it couldn't be his charm.

Still, there was a soothing quality about the rancher. He was never in her road, always ready to wait upon her, anxious always for her safety and comfort.

You could not have everything in a man, of course, but still, when one thought of dark-eyed Spanish dons and honeyed words and extravagant promises, one might occasionally sigh.

Susan Price was not very tall, but what she lacked in stature she made up in flame. Her hair was shimmering gold and her spirit—call it temper—went with that shade. She was kind and compassionate to a fault but she could also soar to heights of rage which terrified beholders. Her one passion in life was championing underdogs, taking this from her father's successful career and making a sort of hobby of it.

She got bored rather easily and just now, riding along the hot road and watching a cloud of dust approach a few miles away, she was very bored. Nothing ever happened in Rio Carlos. It was, of course, rather wild at times, and outlaws had been increasingly frequent of late, but that was not really anything to interest a girl. Her father, Sam Price, had bought a spread here after ailing lungs had retired him from his great practice. It was healthy, but that was all Susan could say for the place when she got this way.

The dust cloud grew taller and at last she could make out the horsemen before it. She checked the sorrel and waited until they came up.

In the vanguard rode Big Bill Bailey, very dusty, but reserved as always and most courteous. He raised his hat over his head and pulled up. Behind him the posse stopped. Spick Murphy was riding in the center, arms tied to his sides, a bloody bandage around his head. His dark eyes were very sad and beseeching as he looked at Susan. He made a helpless, forlorn figure in that bristling multitude.

"I guess," said Big Bill carefully, "that the country will be safer now. We got Spick Murphy."

She looked at Spick and he grew sadder than ever, hanging his head.

"All of you against that one man?" said the unpredictable Susan.

"Sure," said Con Mathews. "You don't think we want to get ourselves killed any more than necessary, do you?"

"What's he done?" said Susan, touching the brim of her little flat sombrero and studying Spick curiously.

"You know Spick Murphy's reputation, ma'am," said Sheriff Doyle.

"He's been rustling stock," said Big Bill.

"And we're going to hang him as soon as we can get a trial," chimed Con.

"I see you've already decided upon a hanging before the trial," said Susan.

"He's guilty, ain't he?" said Doyle.

"I'm sure I wouldn't know. Judges and juries usually decide those things. Or do they?"

They might have been warned by her mild, only slightly sarcastic tone. They knew a few of the things she had done around there but they were too flushed with victory to pay any heed to a mere girl.

"Shore they do," said Doyle. "But when you get killers and rustlers like this gent, there ain't much question about it. He's changed his last brand and shot his last man, miss, and there'll be one less outlaw to trouble peaceful citizens. I saw my duty and it's done."

Doyle thought this was a pretty impressive campaign speech

*"All of you against that one man?"*
*said the unpredictable Susan.*

# GET 4 FREE BOOKS!

You can have the titles in the Stories from the Golden Age delivered to your door by signing up for the book club. Start today, and we'll send you **4 FREE BOOKS** (worth $39.80) as your reward.

◄◦►

The collection includes 80 volumes (book or audio) by master storyteller L. Ron Hubbard in the genres of science fiction, fantasy, mystery, adventure and western, originally penned for the pulp magazines of the 1930s and '40s.

◄◦►

## YES! ☐

Sign me up for the Stories from the Golden Age Book Club and send me my first book for $9.95 with my **4 FREE BOOKS** (FREE shipping). I will pay only $9.95 each month for the subsequent titles in the series. Shipping is FREE and I can cancel any time I want to.

First Name _____ Middle Name _____ Last Name _____

Address _____

City _____ State _____ ZIP _____

Telephone _____ E-mail _____

Credit/Debit Card #: _____

Card ID# (last 3 or 4 digits): _____ Exp Date: _____ / _____

Date (month/day/year) _____ / _____ / _____

Signature: _____

Comments: _____

Check here ✔ to receive a FREE Stories from the Golden Age catalog or go to: **GoldenAgeStories.com**.

*Thank you!*

and he made a mental note of it for future reference—until he saw its effect upon Susan.

"Without trial, you have already decided to hang him!" blazed Susan. "Fifteen men against one! You ought to be ashamed to call yourselves human beings."

The posse blinked as one man.

"You've decided he's guilty already. Have you any *proof*? Fifteen men against one! How do you know?" She looked just like her lawyer father.

"Well, everybody knows—" began Big Bill.

"Public opinion doesn't convict a man. And by law, a man is innocent until he is proven guilty. Did *you* ever see him rustle any stock?"

"Well . . . no. But—"

"There! You don't know whether he's guilty or not! You saw how sad he looked and how he was wounded and at the mercy of those men. He knows he's going to his death and yet he isn't whining about it."

"Sure not," said Big Bill, frowning. "He knows he's got it coming, doesn't he?"

"Bah! Can't you *think*?"

"Why, sure, but—"

"Why, sure, but—" she mimicked. "You talk and act and eat like one of those beeves of yours! Haven't you any kindness? No mercy? How do you know he's guilty? 'Everybody knows.' Don't you have any ideas of your own?"

She was being unjust and knew it, but all day she had been bored.

69

Big Bill froze like a snowcapped peak and just sat there staring at her.

Finally she said, "Bah!" and quirted her sorrel and rode away with angry speed.

Big Bill watched her go with a puzzled scowl. He took off his John B. and scratched his head. "She's been that way before and tomorrow she'll forget it. But how anybody could see anything in Spick Murphy . . ." To the posse he said, "Come on."

She was very aloof when they passed her.

# Chapter Three

MATTERS might have remained in that state without further trouble if Susan had not needed a few groceries for Sam Price's supper. But she did and her future was changed by two cans of corn, a steak and a pound of coffee.

She stopped before the San Carlos General Store and swung down, throwing her reins over the hitch rack. There was considerable talk going on both inside and outside the store. Old Bus Hansey, who had been with Major Reno, was whittling with great agitation and using up plug tobacco at an alarming rate.

And just as Susan mounted the steps, Old Bus creaked, "I tell ye, Lon, there ain't no sense wastin' the taxpayers' money on no trial. Why, I recollect the day when the sheriff was expected to do his own killin'. We're gittin' soft! They hain't been but one murder for a month and—"

Lon brought his chair down on all four legs. "Con says there ain't goin' to be no mistake this time. And Doyle reckons there won't be no lynchin'! What's the difference? They'll hang him on say-so and that's enough fer me."

Susan had stopped at the top of the steps and they both saw her. Old Bus touched a gnarled finger to his battered hat, about to speak a greeting to her.

But Susan was suddenly angry again. She had a streak in her which made her champion any underdog—the same streak which had made her father a great criminal lawyer.

"You ought to be ashamed of yourselves!" she said hotly. "How do you know he's guilty?"

Everybody on the store porch looked startled. Old Bus shifted his chaw. "Why, miss, you won't find a Mex or a white man in the Rio Carlos basin but what kin think up somethin' mean about Spick Murphy. He's the killin'est, lowest, ornery, most—"

"Say-so!" said Susan. "Public opinion! Rumor! And you call yourselves thinking men! You'll see that he hangs just because you believe he's guilty."

Amazement stopped all activity of knives and sticks. These elder and somewhat shiftless citizens had only known Susan for a few years, but in that time she had once taken her quirt to a hard case for beating a horse; she had, single-handed, stopped a sheep-cattle war by the very weight of her fury and scorn; she had done a number of surprising things. But to hear her champion a man she knew nothing about, and that man Spick Murphy . . . ! Well!

She favored them all with a glare and forgot about her groceries. She turned and went swiftly along the boardwalk to the nearby weather-beaten jail.

Sheriff Doyle, big and hearty and red of face, was sitting with his feet on his desk, content after his long morning ride. He saw Susan and quickly lowered his feet and took off his hat.

"Howdy, miss."

She wanted no preliminaries. "They're talking about lynching your prisoner, Spick Murphy."

"Shore now, miss, they'll always talk. Gives them somethin' to do. I will say, though, that it wouldn't be much loss if they did."

"What? You'd let them have him?"

Doyle sensed a cyclone. "See here, miss, I never thought a good, sweet girl like you would stand up for a killer like Spick."

"I'd stand up for anybody who hasn't a chance of justice. Trial! You won't give him a trial. Regardless of evidence, you'll hang him if he isn't lynched first."

"Shore, miss, I appreciate your interest in justice, seein' as how your pappy is who he is. But this country is different, miss. We got a pack of outlaws in Rio Carlos and we got to trim 'em down. If we make an example out of Spick—"

"Example! Then you haven't even the honesty of knowing his guilt. There's been rustling, there's been killing, certainly. But the state has no right—"

"Now, miss, you better go talk to your pappy before you start blowin' up about this."

"May I see the prisoner?"

"Why . . . Gosh, I—"

"Is there any reason why I can't?"

"No, but . . ." He gave up and got his keys and she followed him back to the cells. He unlocked the outer door and let her pass and then locked it after her and sat down in the backless chair.

Spick Murphy was not feeling so well. He had a headache

from the bullet crease over his ear and he knew that a noose would soon put a stop to that. He felt very greatly wronged, as no bad man ever really believes himself bad.

He came to the bars and saw Susan and the hunted look went out of his eyes to be replaced by the most saintly expression imaginable.

"I saw them bringing you in," said Susan.

"Yes'm. They caught up with me in the Cordilleras and I never would have been caught if I hadn't stopped to help a sick Mexican."

"A sick Mexican?"

"Yes'm. The poor fellow had hurt his ankle in a fall from the horse he was riding and when I passed him in the trail, I couldn't leave him there for the wolves, could I?"

"You knew they were after you?"

"Yes'm. I could see their dust, but the Mexican—"

"Why were you running away?"

"Oh, I know there's been a lot of talk. And when a friend of mine told me that they were after me, I knew I wouldn't have a chance, no matter how innocent I was. So I tried to get away."

"You've been in jail before?"

"No, *ma'am*!"

"Why did they single you out as their game?"

"Well, ma'am, there's been quite a bit of rustling going on what with Con Mathews tryin' to keep from going broke and they had to pick on *somebody*. And since I stopped Con Mathews from shooting a Mexican woman in cold blood—"

"When did that happen?"

"Didn't you hear about it, ma'am? But then, of course, Con Mathews wouldn't ever tell about it, what with all the things he and Big Bill Bailey have done to rid the range of sheep. Not that they're bad, ma'am, and Big Bill is a nice fellow, but sheep and cattle just don't mix, and neither do Indians and whites. You really want to know why they got me, ma'am?"

"Yes."

"Well, you knew I was half-Apache and half-Irish, didn't you?"

"No."

"Well, I am. And nobody around here ever had any use for me. The Indians wouldn't have anything to do with me because I was half-white and the whites won't have anything to do with me because I'm half-Indian and nobody ever let me hold a job very long. After I got an education in the mission school, I had just nothing but trouble every place I went because the big cattlemen wouldn't let the Mexicans alone and the sheepmen keep driving out the small ranchers, and honest, ma'am, I can't stand around and see things like that happen all the time."

"Of course not!"

"But there's no use wasting any sympathy upon me, ma'am. I'm done for. A lynch mob or the law will hang me. But God is the only one who can judge me. And when I stand before His Great Judgment Seat, I shall not be afraid."

He almost broke down at this point and his handsome

face was sad but brave. "To help those who need help is no crime in His eyes, ma'am, and I have done only that which I considered right. Waste no sympathy. The will of the crowd will be done."

Susan was touched. Her face hardened into determination. "Don't give up hope. I'll find a way to help you."

# Chapter Four

WHEN Susan Price got back to the ranch she found Big Bill sitting on the top step with her eight-year-old brother, Buster. Big Bill was demonstrating the border shift to an apt pupil when he heard Susan. He thrust his .45 into its holster and took off his hat as he stood up.

Buster looked reproachfully around Big Bill's right leg. "Hell," said Buster. "I was just gettin' the hang of it and *you* had to come along."

"Buster!" said Susan.

"Awright. Heck, then."

"Ma'am," said Big Bill, "I'm glad to see you got home all right. I was wondering . . ."

"Thank you," said Susan.

"Ma'am, I was wondering if you still felt sorry for that polecat, Spick Murphy. I got to thinking about it and remembering the way he's got with the women and—"

"Sir?"

"Well, you got mixed up in a sheep war and I thought if you was goin' to get mixed up in this, I better try to ride you off. Spick's goin' to be lynched and that's all there is to it. I—"

"You are convinced of that, are you?" said Susan icily.

"Shore. Everybody knows—"

"You're willing to condemn a man before he's even tried!

You despise him because he's half-Indian and half-white! You're just like the rest of these barbarous men! The poor fellow hasn't a chance of a fair trial! Get out of my sight!"

Big Bill didn't move. He was too stunned. He stood revolving his hat round and round while Susan entered the house. Finally, very puzzled, he went out and climbed his horse and rode disconsolately away.

Sam Price heard the hoofbeats and glanced out of his study window. He sat up straight and laid John Marshall aside. Susan came in.

"What's the matter with Big Bill?" said Sam Price. "He looked pretty sad. Have a fight?"

"He's a fool!" said Susan.

Sam Price leaned back in the Morris chair. "So you did have a fight. What about?"

Susan sat down on the arm of his chair and ran her fingers thoughtfully through his sparse gray locks. "Dad, you've got to do me a favor."

Sam Price suspected something was coming and he knew there wasn't much use trying to fight it. The very futility of the effort caused his jaw to set in a hostile manner.

"If it's more Mexicans and sheep, I am telling you positively that I am not interested. These matters are in the hands of the men they concern and my jurisdiction ends with the front door."

"Now, Dad," said Susan.

"Don't you 'Now, Dad' me, Susan Price. My mind is made up. I don't care what has happened, I won't be a party to it and that's final."

Gruffly he sat back again and pulled John Marshall into his lap and began to open the pages. There was a long silence and then in a high-pitched, angry voice he demanded, "Well, dammit, what is it?"

"They caught a man named Spick Murphy and they're determined to hang him as a rustler and murderer as an example to the outlaws in Rio Carlos. He's a fine-looking young fellow, half-Apache, half-Irish. . . ."

"Too many outlaws around here anyway," said Sam. "Anything that isn't nailed down turns up missing. See here, young woman, I have definitely retired and nothing short of an earthquake could get me in front of a jury box again. I refuse to have anything to do with it!"

Again he turned to John Marshall and turned a few more pages.

"Well," he demanded, explosively. "What chance has he got?"

"None," replied Susan. "Without real evidence, they are determined that he is going to die."

"Without real evidence? Why, that's . . . But no! No, dammit, you're not going to get me into a courtroom over a half-breed. You've been reading out of my library. I *know* you have. You haven't been the same since you read Elizabeth Fry on prison reform and crime! To hell with Elizabeth Fry!"

He got up, almost knocking her off the arm of his chair. He advanced across the room and poured a drink.

"Well? What's public opinion got against him?"

"They're going to make him suffer for every crime which has been committed in San Carlos and Rio Carlos."

"Huh," said Sam. "He couldn't have done all of them. Not fair to make one man pay the whole cost. . . . No! I won't defend him! I won't have anything to do with him! I tell you I have retired!"

And so it was that Sam Price stood in the San Carlos courtroom the following month, defending Spick Murphy on the charge of rustling and murder.

And Sam Price *was* Sam Price, and though Con Mathews had been most diligent in capturing Spick Murphy in the Cordilleras and though Sheriff Doyle had long been on the trail of the defendant, it soon became clear to all that both men had been most lamentably careless about collecting concrete evidence.

And because Sam Price *was* Sam Price, even the prejudiced jury could not bring in a conviction and Spick Murphy, meek and mild, was again released upon the world.

# Chapter Five

B IG BILL BAILEY, resplendent in a sombrero which would have looked small on the Sphinx and generally dressed up to please the feminine eye, was waiting outside the courthouse when the jailer loosed Spick Murphy.

Sam Price, still garbed in the black and the dignity of the court, and Susan were there, waiting. The loafers from the San Carlos General Store were standing around and recollecting a time when nothing like this would have been permitted to happen.

Big Bill thought the moment propitious to sign an armistice with Susan. He had, of course, delivered blunt testimony in the court against Spick Murphy's character, but that had been purely in the line of business and a war to Big Bill was over when it was lost or won.

He approached and raised his hat courteously, "Mister Price, sir, I wish to congratulate you on your case. I've heard a lot about how you worked, sir, but it wasn't anything to the seeing. Even if you did hornswoggle that yellow Gila monster's freedom, I—"

"I might object to the word," said Sam with a grin, "but I won't. Thanks, Bailey."

"Susan," said Big Bill, turning, hat still in the air above his head as a sort of umbrella, "may I invite you to go for a ride this afternoon?"

Susan looked at him coldly.

"But . . . but I haven't done anything," said Big Bill. "I *had* to give that testimony, didn't I?"

"You almost lost Father the case and Murphy his life," said Susan distantly. "I shall thank you, sir, to stay away from the Pinta."

"Shore, Susan, you wouldn't let a filthy lobo like Murphy come between *us*, would you? He ain't worth it, ma'am. Let's forget about it. The fight's fought and you won. That ought to close the whole deal and call for new cards all around."

His plea might have taken effect. He had planned his wording an hour before he had delivered his speech. But all that labor was lost because, at that moment, Spick Murphy was ejected from the courthouse by disgusted Sheriff Doyle, who thereafter dusted his hands and wiped them on his pants.

Spick Murphy looked very pale after his month in the hoosegow. Further, he looked saintly and repentant. He swept off his hat and bowed so low that the brim touched earth.

"Miss Price," he said with feeling, "how can I ever repay you for your kindness. And Mr. Price, whatever charges you care to make for your services I shall labor for years if necessary to repay."

"Hell," said Sam Price. "You don't owe me anything, sonny."

"But," faltered Spick, "I heard your fees were enormous. Fifty thousand . . . a hundred thousand . . ."

"Right. But as I won't take less and you could never pay it, write it off to experience. Susan, I think we had better be leaving."

But she lingered, looking at repentant Spick Murphy. "What are you going to do now?"

"I don't know," said Spick. "No one here would ever give me honest employment and I have no other home. Perhaps if I wandered to far countries . . ."

"You'll do nothing of the kind," said Susan. "You can show your appreciation to my father by helping him at the ranch. He needs another hand."

"I what?" said Sam Price.

"You know you do!" said Susan.

"I guess I do," surrendered Sam.

"I should like nothing better," said Spick. "I shall get some of my belongings together and report for my orders this evening."

"That will be fine," said Susan.

Sam was dragging her away before anything else happened. Spick stood on the steps and smiled after them. Big Bill stood with his hat still raised and stared. He had forgotten to lower his arm. But he remembered now and set his hat back on his head and faced Spick Murphy.

Big Bill figured out what he would do and that gave Spick a chance to ease away a foot or two. Big Bill advanced and again Spick retreated. Abruptly Spick found himself backed up to the hitch rack. Big Bill's big hand held him there, containing a quantity of shirt.

*Abruptly Spick found himself backed up to the
hitch rack. Big Bill's big hand held him there,
containing a quantity of shirt.*

"You wormed yourself into this," said Big Bill. "And I can't do what I'd like to do without getting into trouble with her. But . . ."

Spick was not a coward by far, but he had the good sense to remain silent and not grin.

"But if I hear of you misbehaving," said Big Bill, "I'll track you to hell and back and when I find you I'll cut off your ears and fry them for breakfast. You got that down pat?"

Spick nodded.

Big Bill released his shirt and stalked over to his horse and left Spick grinning to himself.

# Chapter Six

SPICK MURPHY was received very badly at first among the punchers of the Pinta spread. Warily they waited for him to do something which would justify their plea that he be fired.

None of them would have dreamed of actually treating Spick Murphy with anything but ginger courtesy. The man was not armed, visibly, but nobody was willing to take a chance with a fellow who could and had driven spikes with bullets at thirty paces.

It was not merely that Spick Murphy was known to be chain lightning with a gun, it was another quality which worried these worthy waddies.

Spick looked like a kid in his teens with a cherubic smile always displayed upon his swarthy face and nothing but kindliness glowing from his Indian black eyes. But physiognomy is the most untrustworthy of sciences and the punchers were not fooled as easily as the naturally impulsive Susan.

They knew that Spick had grinned like that since the day of his birth, even when he was shooting a man in the back. Drunk or sober, angry or in the best of humors, free or jailed, Spick's appearance attested only great camaraderie toward the world.

And that was what made it so bad. You could never tell when he was really mad or drunk or kill-crazy and therefore it behooved all those endowed with a love of life to walk easily where Spick was concerned.

But that did not prevent the Pinta spread from ignoring him, which they could do collectively and with little personal danger.

After a few weeks, however, their antipathy toward him waned and they began to think that his dangerousness had been greatly overrated. He did those jobs assigned to him with an ease which made everyone else look clumsy, and did them cheerfully. And at the fall roundup, he could be found from dawn until dark beside the branding fire scorching The Paint-Bucket brand into hair and hide. The Pinta punchers forgot themselves so far as to actually admire the artistic way Spick handled a running iron.

It became increasingly apparent that Spick had taken a turn for the better. He never got roostered in San Carlos, he went far out of his way to avoid fights and his attitude toward Sam Price and his daughter was something to behold as a model for all respect and courtesy.

Buster, at first, had been very diffident about Spick and the wise shook their heads and quoted the old saw about "dogs and children." But children, after all, are practically human, and after the roundup, Buster thawed.

This came to a very moody Big Bill Bailey one crisp evening. Big Bill had come to the Pinta with lessening frequency, taking the attitude of a policeman dropping around to a gambling hall he wished he could close.

Buster found Big Bill leaning against the corral and looked up brightly.

"Gimme your gun," ordered Buster.

Big Bill handed it down.

"Look," ordered Buster.

And before he could be stopped, he had fanned the hog leg into the side of the barn, completely knocking out a knot some two inches in diameter. The kick of the gigantic weapon had knocked off his small sombrero and now he picked it up and put it back very solemnly.

"Us gunfighters has got to practice," said Buster.

"Who taught you that?" inquired Big Bill, reloading and looking distrustfully at his former protégé.

"Why, Spick, o' course. Say, he's a swell shot. I bet he's a better shot than even you. I tell you, Bill," added Buster with great gravity, "that guy is hell on wheels and no brakes when it comes to shootin'."

Naturally, Big Bill Bailey did not take very well to the statement. Silently he stared at Buster and then shoved his gun back in its holster. He wanted very badly to tell Buster a few pertinent facts but he felt very inadequate to the task.

Miserably Big Bill crawled his bronc and went away from there.

"I'll tell Sis you was here!" shouted Buster after him. His little forehead wrinkled in a puzzled frown. He looked around but could find no elders nearby. Accordingly he spat into the dust and muttered, "Wonder what the hell's wrong with him?"

He turned then and was so startled he put daylight between his boots and earth.

Spick had slid around the end of the barn, his face very calm, a .45 in his hand.

"Whatcha want to scare me for?" complained Buster.

Spick looked around and relaxed, shoving the .45 inside his shirt.

"I didn't know you carried a gun like that, Spick."

"What was the shooting about, kid?"

"Aw, I was just showin' Big Bill Bailey how handy I was with a shootin' iron. And I showed him, too! Look at the knot over there, partner."

Spick grinned as he looked at the 'dobe-lumber side of the structure. The bullet group was very good indeed, but there was something else causing Spick's grin.

He went back to the door and looked in and there on the floor, very, very dead, lay a prize milk cow. Buster's slugs made a very fine pattern under her ear.

"Oh," whispered Buster, faintly. "I . . . I better be gettin' out of here, Spick. I . . . I don't think Sis will like that."

And when the deed was discovered several hours later, Susan was not at all pleased. Buster was ordered to bed without any supper and, adding insult to it, was told he could not leave said house for a week.

When Susan came out of the front room and into the dusk, she found Spick sitting on the top step braiding a rope. He looked at her very disarmingly.

"I wouldn't be too hard on him, Miss Price. It was my fault. Honest it was."

"You're trying to cover him," accused Susan.

"Well, maybe. But just the same, Miss Price, it was I that taught him how to shoot like that. And if I say it myself, I was nine before I could make a group like that. Someday he'll maybe need that training to protect his own home, his own wife and children. There's been a lot of men who would be alive today if they had spent a little more time with a target."

It was like Spick to add such a happy, homely note to the affair. He could not now be censored and told that he was practically inviting Buster to launch himself as a gun terror in his teens.

"It makes no difference," said Susan. "I've talked to Father to try and make him forbid Buster to touch guns, but it's no use. If Mother were still here, *she* wouldn't stand for it. I . . . I won't be hard on you about it, Spick. You know all about such things and you put too high a value on them. But please don't encourage Buster. It's not that I care anything about a cow, but what if it had been a man?"

This, naturally, made very small impression on Spick Murphy. In fact, he could have shown her definitely that a cow on the hoof was worth a lot more than most men, according to his lights. But he had something else to say.

"I wouldn't have kept it up, Miss Price, if he hadn't persisted himself. But Big Bill Bailey showed him a few tricks like the border shift and the Curly Bill Spin and the pinwheel, but his hands are so small and guns are so heavy, I figured he'd better not be foolin' with them unless he knew they'd shoot, too. And naturally when Big Bill Bailey dropped in and wouldn't believe Buster, the kid showed him—"

91

"Big Bill was here today?"

"Yes'm. He was here. He came cat-footing around. I guess he's trying to keep an eye on me."

"That's ridiculous," said Susan.

"Maybe so, Miss Price, but Big Bill Bailey has a lot of trouble getting an idea out of his head once it's stuck there. Hello, there comes Mr. Price from town."

Sam Price pulled up the buckboard before the porch and threw the reins to Spick. He climbed out, brushing the dust from his coat and looking very satisfied with himself.

"Father," said Susan, "Buster . . ."

"Give them a good rubdown," said Sam to Spick. "They've been hitting it up pretty hard. Yes, Susie? What about Buster?"

He went up the porch and Susan followed him inside. "He shot at the barn and killed Lulu. He didn't do it on purpose, really he didn't, and I've already punished him by sending him to bed and telling him he had to stay in for a week."

"He what?" said Sam.

"He shot Lulu through the side of the barn with a revolver. Big Bill dared him to and he did. I've already punished him. . . ."

"There's no saving the cow?"

"All six bullets hit her just under the ear, poor thing. She never made a sound, according to Buster. I had to tell you because you'd miss Lulu and the boys dragged her out on the mesa for the coyotes. He didn't mean—"

"How far away was he?"

"Why . . . just over by the corral."

"Fifty or sixty feet anyway," said Sam. "All six in a small bunch? How big was it?"

"About two inches. I've already punished him so you needn't—"

"Punish him? Hell, Susie, what do I care about a cow? Say, that lad is some shot. I wish I could do that well."

"But Lulu cost a lot of money."

"Money," scoffed Sam. "What do I care about money now? As if I didn't have enough already, old Jameson of Jameson vs. Whitlock—you remember the fees I was to get?—well, old Jameson died and his trustees discovered that he had faked his books so I wouldn't get my twenty percent of the settlement. They just shipped the specie to San Carlos. Damned if I know what to do with it. Buy more land and cattle, I guess. Can't let two hundred thousand lie around loose."

"Then you won't punish Buster? I couldn't stand to have you whip him after I sent him to bed. He's been punished enough already."

"If I had my way, I'd give him a sharpshooter medal. But say, what do you know about old Jameson faking those books just to cut me out when they settled out of court, huh? He always was a wily old rat. Wait until . . ."

That was the last Spick Murphy cared to hear about it. He slipped silently off the porch and, as quietly as possible, led the team back toward the barn.

And as he rubbed them down he broke forth into melodious song.

# Chapter Seven

THAT night Buster was restive in his sleep, rolling from one side of the bed to the other at short intervals. The last time he turned that night, he put his small, troubled face into the beam of a bull's-eye lantern.

He was groggily awake on the instant, sitting up, striving to force a yell of terror through his contracted throat.

Spick's voice was as sibilant as a cat's. "Don't make a sound, Buster. It's me—Spick."

The course of the bull's-eye's flickering beam was bent downward to the red Navajo beside the bed. Buster stared at Spick's silhouette in the open window. The curtains were blowing like uneasy white ghosts and Spick was very black in the moonlight. He stepped to Buster's side with a tread lighter than a jaguar's.

"I knew how bad you felt," whispered Spick. "I couldn't stand to hear her ragging you about something you couldn't help."

Buster was awake now, scrubbing his eyes with the backs of his hands, the indignation of great wrong filling him anew.

"Besides, what's a cow," whispered Spick. "I want to help you."

Buster looked attentive.

"I've been wanting to go on a hunting trip in the Cordilleras," said Spick, "and I'm leaving tonight. Maybe if you just vanished for three or four days and made them know how you felt about this, you'd have things coming your way better."

Buster was trying to think and he squinted up his eyes with the effort. He had been in many another such scrape before this and now Spick was conjuring up all those nights without supper. The proposition was attractive.

"What you goin' to hunt?" said Buster, lowering his voice to a mysterious whisper.

"Grizzlies and deer. There's a cabin I know about. I got the supplies we need and I've got a new rifle for you—that is, if you want to go."

"A new rifle?" said Buster eagerly.

"Sssh," cautioned Spick. "They said you couldn't have any more guns but if you bag a grizzly by yourself, maybe they'll have to change their minds, huh? I'm all for you, Buster."

"What kind of a rifle?"

"A Winchester .22 brand-new. It's outside in the packs."

Buster was out on the instant. He swiftly slid into his overalls and grabbed his hat in one hand, his boots in the other and started for the window.

At the sill he whispered, "Maybe I better leave a note. I . . . I don't want Sis to worry *too* much."

"Okay," replied Spick affably.

Buster took his slate and scribbled:

> Sis, I'm going to hunt me a few bears and deer and things with Spick.
>
> Buster

He hung it on the bedpost and then consented to leave. Spick lingered long enough to wipe the writing off on his pants and scrawl an entirely different message thereon.

Very softly they stole past the corral to the four mounts Spick had saddled and packed. They led these for some distance before they mounted.

"First," said Spick, "I got to see a man in town and after that, we're really on our way."

"Swell," said Buster. "Now where's that new Winchester, partner?"

Spick's grin was nothing more than a gleam of teeth in blackness. "I guess that's where I slipped up, kid."

"Say!" said Buster, startled by the grating tone. "What's the matter with you?"

"Never mind what's the matter with me, kid. Ride and keep quiet or I'm giving you a taste of this quirt."

Hanging at the foot of Buster's bed was the slate and upon it uneven letters said:

I collected my pay in San Carlos. Follow me and all you'll find is what's left of your brat.

# Chapter Eight

THE desert dawn lay cold and thin upon the sleeping rancho of Big Bill Bailey. As yet but half visible, the kingly castle of 'dobe showed only a thin blue spire of smoke to mark the efforts of a Chinese beginning breakfast so silently that Big Bill Bailey slumbered peacefully in his throne room.

He was wishing dimly that he had enough presence to get up and pull another blanket over himself but he didn't. With half thoughts coursing slowly through his mind between dreams and ideas, a panorama of his immediate woes began to unfold, now very real, now assuaged by wildly painted hopes which he would not remember upon waking.

A rolling, staccato sound troubled him vaguely. No such running horse should be here on the ranch at this time of the day. But the sound grew louder and louder and then stopped, was gone for an instant to be immediately taken up and continued by the swift patting of boots on sand and then on wood. That stopped too and even yet Big Bill was giving it no real thought.

He heard Wang's singsong voice, "Him sleepy. No can see, missee."

And then Susan's urgent words, "I've *got* to see him. Quick!"

Big Bill heard that. He rolled over and swung his feet down fishing foggily for his boots. The spurs were cold to his fingers as he brushed them aside and almost immediately stepped on their sharp rowels. The pain brought him more fully awake and he stopped hunting.

Throwing a kingly slicker about him he went to the door and opened it.

Susan was walking swiftly toward him, her big eyes wild with terror.

"Big Bill! Spick's gone! Buster's gone! You've got to do something!"

She had a slate in her hand, shoving it at him.

Big Bill ran his hand over his face to stir up his blood. He rubbed his eyes and became conscious of the slate. He took it and turned it around and read it.

He read it again before it made sense to him. He gave his head a violent shake and came all the way to the surface. "What's this all about?"

"Buster's gone! Spick's gone! You've got to do something!"

She was wringing her hands pitifully, looking expectantly at him.

"Begin at the beginning," said Big Bill. "You don't make sense."

"Spick robbed the San Carlos bank. Don't you see? And then he came back and took Buster so that nobody would follow him. But he'll kill Buster. I know he'll kill him. Maybe he's already dead. You've—"

"Which way did he go?"

"I . . . I don't know."

Big Bill thought for a while and then made a decision. "He

must have hit for the border. That would bring him within three miles of here if he was making it straight, which means he'll be at Coyote Pass."

Big Bill was wide awake now and his stare was level and sober upon her. "Until you needed me," he said slowly, "you forgot all about me."

"Yes," she said swiftly, not hearing him. "Yes, of course. We've got to go if we catch them at all."

"Until you had something for me to do," said Big Bill, "I was so much sagebrush. You threw me over for Spick Murphy, a killer."

"Yes— No! No! He meant nothing. Believe me, he meant nothing to me. I tried to be decent to him because I thought everybody was his enemy. I'm sorry. I'll do anything! But for God's sake, Big Bill, don't stand here talking. Can't you realize he'll murder Buster?"

"I know," said Big Bill. "But what makes you think I'll do this for you? Why should I?"

She looked at him blankly, unable to fully understand that this was Big Bill Bailey talking. Big Bill Bailey, the most dependable man in Rio Carlos, the righter of wrongs, king of the desert ranges. . . .

"You got yourself into this against my advice," said Big Bill. "Now you come to me to get you out of it when you could have saved yourself all this trouble. Your crusade for Spick Murphy's come back at you. You think I'm easy. You think I'm thick-skulled. Until you need me you have nothing to do with me. And if I do this for you, it will change nothing. Why should I go out there and match guns with Spick Murphy just as a favor to a woman who calls me only when she has a dirty job to be done?"

He said it without rancor, only as a series of questions which seemed also to be troubling him. If he had been angry she could have matched him and derided him for a coward or anything else. But the chill of his tones and the knowledge that her brother was in danger gave her a beaten attitude.

"You mean you won't?" she said brokenly.

"I didn't say that. But I certainly won't walk into a mess like this for nothing."

"You mean . . . you mean you want money?"

"What use have I got for that?"

She could not understand this. She was shivering with both the cold and the inner quake of fear for Buster.

Big Bill's tone was suddenly harsh. "Why don't you go for Sheriff Doyle? Why not let a posse take out after them? Why come here and ask me to take on a killer single-handed?"

She was crying now. "You know why. They . . . they wouldn't risk anything to save Buster. They'd pen him up and he'd shoot Buster. . . . I know he would. . . ."

"And so you come to me and ask that I invite sudden death . . . I'd hardly fight that buzz saw for nothing."

"What do you want?"

"If I do this for you," said Big Bill in a hard voice, "will you marry me?"

She straightened up. Something like contempt crept into her glance. "You'd force me?"

"I hold the winning hand," said Big Bill, jerking his thumb

102

at his holstered gun which dangled from a peg. "And I mean to play it."

"All right. All right, I'll marry you if you do this."

Big Bill looked at her for several seconds as though deciding whether or not she would keep her word. Then he turned and closed the door in her face, to emerge a few minutes later fully dressed and buckling on his Colt.

"While they're saddling a couple horses," said Big Bill, "I'll take some coffee. Have some?"

She did not answer him, pressing herself back against the wall as he passed her.

# Chapter Nine

IT was noon when Big Bill Bailey and Susan Price thundered down the steep slope into the southern end of Coyote Pass. The white-flecked mounts showed the difficulty of the byway they had traversed to short-circuit their route.

Big Bill pulled to a skidding halt at the side of the trail which swept back obliquely from them and looked down at the undisturbed dust.

"No tracks made since last night's wind," announced Big Bill after due process of thought. "They either didn't take this route or we're ahead of them."

Susan was wrapped in the dust cloud of her own making which had now caught up with her. Her small face was framed by her black, flat hat now turned to the white shade of alkali, chin thong still tight against her small jaw. Fearfully she looked up at the rearing heights of the fantastic rocks about them.

"This is Mexico," said Big Bill, "but we're not going to worry about that. What the Feds don't know won't hurt them and Spick won't be expecting this. He's most likely camped up one of these draws."

Susan still had nothing to say. The dust had cleared and the sun beat unmercifully down upon her checkered shirt.

She was still sweeping the towering badlands with worried gaze.

Big Bill tensed and raised his head. "There! Do you smell that wood smoke?"

"No."

"Open your mouth and take a slow, easy breath. There, smell it?"

She looked at him in sudden fright. "He's close by."

"Maybe. Maybe not." Big Bill got down and whipped his reins over his horse's head, dropping them. From his scabbard he pulled his Winchester.

It was not quite out of the boot when Spick's mocking voice came down to them. "Put it back, Bailey. You haven't got a chance."

Susan whipped around and stared upward, trembling hand on her horn. Spick was a black silhouette against the sky not fifty feet away, a silver-mounted six-gun alertly held at his hip. His white teeth were bared in a grin.

Big Bill had stopped like a statue, the Winchester poised with its muzzle still inside the boot.

"This is nice of you, Bailey," said Spick. "I couldn't figure out how to get the lady too and now you've solved it for me. Come up here, kid."

This last was addressed to Buster. Spick knelt and grabbed the boy by his collar and hauled up, standing him in front.

"I tried to yell at you," whimpered Buster. "Honest I did. . . . But—"

"Shut up," snapped Spick with a cuff.

Susan could see now why Buster had not yelled. His mouth was a red splotch of fresh blood where a gun barrel had struck him. The hypodermic of rage steeled Susan.

"Leave him alone!"

"Don't try for that gun," said Spick amiably. "Not if you want to live."

Susan stayed her hand and looked urgently at Big Bill's back. The man had not moved a fraction of an inch. Contempt came into Susan's face.

"This was too easy," said Spick. "An Apache in his cradle could have figured out what you'd do, where you'd cross, how long it would take you. A squaw would have known that no posse would come over the border. And I don't have to tell you that there's no Mexican patrol that can't be bought. That should demonstrate the superiority of brains over brawn, Bailey."

"Are you going to . . . to kill him?" said Buster.

"Turn around, Bailey. I never shot a man in the back in my life."

"Don't!" screamed Susan.

Big Bill was turning around. A six-gun at fifty paces could not miss in the able hands of Spick Murphy and the six-gun was already cocked.

The Winchester swooped out of its boot as Big Bill spun, sun flashing from his cartridge belt, small swirls of dust shooting out from under his boots.

He got completely turned and the Winchester was coming up.

Spick fired with the cool deliberation of a marksman. The

bullet kicked Big Bill back into the roan's flank. The mount's sudden start at both blow and shot knocked Big Bill forward and flat.

Spick's second shot ricocheted from a stone beside Big Bill's face.

And out of the curling dust blazed the Winchester.

Spick dropped his six-gun. He put both hands to his face and the blood came oozing through his fingers. He stood there, wavering, and Buster scuttled to one side. Unsteadily Spick took a pace forward, out over nothingness.

Slowly the dust settled again. The roan stopped a hundred feet away and looked wonderingly back, having stepped on his reins.

Susan leaped down and sped to Big Bill's side but before she got there he was sitting up.

The stock of the Winchester was cleanly split and a long scarlet furrow ran up his shoulder.

Susan stopped when she saw he was all right and then reached down as though to help him to his feet. He shook her off and pulled himself over to a rock. Methodically he took off his silk neckerchief and began to bind his own shoulder with his hand and his teeth.

Buster scrambled down from his high perch and came running. "Gee! Gee, you were lucky! He hit your gun!"

Big Bill's voice was muffled by his mouthful of silk but it was still matter-of-fact. "He never failed to shoot for the heart in his life. That ain't luck, Buster."

Susan had control of herself again and she clutched Buster

to her, much against his liking. "How . . . how can I ever thank you?"

Big Bill looked sideways at her. "You remember your promise?"

She did. It jolted her. "I didn't think . . ."

"It was a promise, wasn't it?"

"Yes. Yes. I'll . . . I'll go through with it."

"You'll marry me because I made you say you would?"

"Yes . . . yes, I'll . . . marry you."

"You sound like those words choked you," said Big Bill, patting his knot in place. "Well, they needn't. Climb your horse and beat it back to your Pinta. I didn't have any intention of holding you."

Amazement, even relief, dawned upon her face as she crouched there beside Buster. "You mean you'll release me from that promise?"

"Sure," said Big Bill bitterly. "Sure I'll release you. I'd pull up stakes and head for Cheyenne before I'd keep my part of it. I'd sell my spread for a plugged *centavo* before I'd ever call you my wife."

The hardness in his voice brought her erect, angered her.

He went steadily on. "All you wanted from me was a favor. I suppose you'd have married Doyle or Con Mathews or anybody if they'd made you promise. If you had any self-respect you never would have consented, that's a cinch. And now I know just how much you think you're worth. I know just where I stand with you. Well, I don't admire the answer, Miss Susan Price, and I wouldn't have the likes of you with ten

thousand beeves thrown in to boot. Now get on your horse
and get out of here, I'm sick of looking at you."

"You . . . you knew you wouldn't go through with this from
the first?"

"Shut up and get out of my sight," said Big Bill. "You make
me sick. I'll recover the money and the horses. Go on! Beat it!"

She did not move. She stood and shook with the violence
of her anger. "You . . . you did this to make me look cheap!"

"That's what you are. Cheap! You aren't worth fighting
for. You're fickle and you're dumb and you haven't got a lick
of sense in that pretty head of yours. I let myself be on call
to you for years but that's through. I never want to see you
again, but if I do I'll quirt you. Now get out."

Still she did not move. The bandage had slipped when he
had waved his arm toward her horse and he winced as he
restored it.

"You don't mean that, Big Bill."

"Mean it? Hell, yes, I mean it. You made a fool out of me
for a damned bandit and that's enough of a dose for anybody
to take for any kind of a cure. Well, I'm cured. For years I've
been tipping my hat and saying 'Yes, ma'am to a woman that
didn't rate a slap from a sheepherder. You figured you were
doing me a hell of a big favor to promise me you'd marry me.
Well, by God, I wouldn't have you around my house if you
came with more gold than you could carry. Get out!"

She stepped closer to him. "You . . . you don't mean that,
Big Bill."

"Mean it? Hell, yes, I mean it! This shoulder is making
me sick enough without having to look at you." He started

up but the effort shifted the bandage again and he sank back, pain in his eyes.

"You need me," she said softly. "Don't send me away. Here, let me tie—"

"Keep your hands off me!" cried Big Bill. "I'd bleed to death before I'd let you touch me."

But she did touch him. She untied his clumsy knot and fixed the tourniquet right, winding it up with a rifle bullet.

He glared at her. Buster looked on in shocked amazement. He had never seen his sister that humbled before.

Big Bill suffered the treatment and apparently decided to let her stick around for the moment.

"Go get my horse," he said gruffly.

She went and got his horse.

"Now scramble around up there and find his camp and saddle his horses and get that money he had. Go on. Snap into it."

She went away and a half-hour later came back with the mounts.

Very sternly he said, "All right. Give me a hand while I mount and we'll get going."

She gave him a hand and let him ride up the trail ahead of her as she and Buster led the rest of the string.

Big Bill turned around in his saddle with a terrifying glare. "We're going right on into San Carlos."

"Yes," said Susan.

"And we'll get there before dark if we push along. So don't lag."

"Yes, Big Bill."

"And when we get there, don't go wandering off anyplace before I can find the justice of the peace. Understand? You'll spend tonight out at my ranch and as long as you behave yourself and quit monkeying around with bandits, you can stay. Do you get that?"

"Yes, Big Bill," said Susan.

# Story Preview

# Story Preview

NOW that you've just ventured through some of the captivating tales in the Stories from the Golden Age collection by L. Ron Hubbard, turn the page and enjoy a preview of *The Toughest Ranger*. Join gun-shy cowboy Petey McGuire, who's been kicked around all of his life. Faced with starvation, he bluffs his way into a job with the rough-n'-tumble Arizona Rangers. But when he's chosen to hunt the most dangerous desperado in the state, Petey's forced to discover what it really means to be Ranger-tough.

# The Toughest Ranger

H E did not know how far he went as his legs were numb and walking, mechanical. But when he looked up he was on the outskirts of a small pueblo. The biggest building in it was a fort-like 'dobe structure which presented an arched gate to the road. There was a sign about that gate: "THE ARIZONA RANGERS."

Petey stopped, hardly seeing the sign at all. In this town, he knew, he could swab out a bar for food. He could clean up a stable. . . .

But Pat had to have shoes and oats and a few weeks' rest.

He turned and looked at the weary little cow pony who didn't even raise his head. Pat pushed ahead a staggering step and shoved his muzzle into Petey's chest.

"Yeah," said Petey. "Yeah. I know. I'm hungry too."

He went toward a saloon and wrapped Pat's reins about the hitchrack. Petey stepped through the doors and into the dim interior.

The bartender was a thick-jowled fellow, shining up glasses. He took one look at Petey and marked him for what he was—saddle tramp.

"Beat it," said the bartender before Petey had spoken. "We got a swamper. There ain't no room in Cristobal for saddle tramps."

"Look," pleaded Petey.

"Yeah, but you better do the lookin'. Captain Shannon locks up every man that can't pay his way. He's cleanin' up the country, see? He's tough, the toughest Ranger in the state and you better take my tip. Beat it."

"You mean . . . you mean just because I'm broke he'd lock me up?" said Petey.

"Well? Why not?"

A chill of terror shook Petey. He turned around and went out into the street. He stopped with Pat's reins in his hand and stared at the big 'dobe building which was marked with the sign: "THE ARIZONA RANGERS."

He knew what he faced. If they locked him up, Pat . . . He hadn't realized until now how shabby Pat looked after a thousand miles. They wouldn't take care of Pat.

But he couldn't go on. No, he couldn't take to the desert again. That way lay death. And here was death for Pat.

His hand was shaking as he pulled his hat brim down. He had no solution for this. Captain Shannon was tough, toughest Ranger in the state. . . .

Petey swallowed hard.

If Pat . . .

Suddenly he wanted to hit somebody, anybody. He wanted to lash out and slay these ghosts which had stalked him for twenty-four years. His rage began to mount.

They had no right to do this to him. No right to kill Pat by loosing him on the waterless desert. Pat needed care!

Suddenly Petey McGuire felt cold. His wits felt like crystal in his head. He was not shaking. He had felt himself grow taller and the experience did not even surprise him. His young face was set and his blue eyes were suddenly hard.

They couldn't kill Pat.

And he knew what he could do.

It was an amazingly brazen idea.

Without any volition of his own he found himself leading Pat across the road and to the 'dobe fort's gate.

Petey was without any fear of anything. He was five times bigger than the sentry.

Maybe it was the sun. Maybe it was starvation. Maybe it was the thought of losing his only friend.

But Petey snapped at the leather-faced sentry, "Where's Shannon?"

He did not recognize his own voice.

The sentry jerked his thumb toward another archway within. Petey, leading Pat, went toward it.

He could see a man beyond. That must be Shannon. A granite boulder behind a desk.

Half of Petey was suddenly scared to death. But the other half of him would not stop walking. He dropped Pat's reins and stalked into the office with a careless, impudent swagger.

Captain Shannon looked up, annoyed, starting to stamp the caller by his dusty, torn clothing.

But Petey was without fear now. Nothing could stop Petey. Not even himself.

"M'name's McGuire," said Petey in a challenging tone. "Petey McGuire. You've heard of me."

Shannon started to make a biting remark, but Petey rushed on without any help from Petey.

"Petey McGuire. From Kansas City to N'Orleans, what I say goes. I'm so tough I'd give a rattler nightmares. You're Shannon and I hear you need tough guys. Well, you ain't got anybody around here that'd stand up to me."

"I don't think . . ." began Shannon sarcastically.

"Hell! You trying to tell me you never heard of Petey McGuire? G'wan, I ain't in no mood for telling funny stories. Where's my badge and where's my bunk? And don't take all day about it!"

Petey was scared down. He was so scared he expected Shannon to leap at him across that battered desk.

But Shannon looked at a dusty, hard-faced, reckless fellow with a twisted grin on his mouth and a swagger in the way he stood.

Shannon was taken not a little aback. He knew his own reputation and now that he was getting old he was guarding it. He had reasons. He had made enemies in his day. And this tough-talking kid had more brass than anybody Shannon had seen for many a year. Shannon's reputation was such as to demand respect. And here was a young whippersnapper . . .

Shannon got up and came around the desk. He was taller than Petey by half a foot and heavier by fifty pounds.

With malice, Shannon said, "So you're tough, are you, sonny?"

Petey startled himself by bristling, "The name's McGuire. Petey McGuire, and if you ain't heard of me you don't know nothin'. Where's the badge and the bunk?"

Shannon scratched his jaw and squinted up a cold, gray

eye. He was amused. But now was not the time. Oh, no. He could read this kid like a book. Youngster putting on a front and nothing more and when the guns began to go . . .

Shannon had a sense of humor.

"Hunter will show you the bunk. We'll see about you later."

To find out more about *The Toughest Ranger* and how you can obtain your copy, go to www.goldenagestories.com.

# Glossary

# Glossary

STORIES FROM THE GOLDEN AGE *reflect the words and expressions used in the 1930s and 1940s, adding unique flavor and authenticity to the tales. While a character's speech may often reflect regional origins, it also can convey attitudes common in the day. So that readers can better grasp such cultural and historical terms, uncommon words or expressions of the era, the following glossary has been provided.*

---

**alkali:** a powdery white mineral that salts the ground in many low places in the West. It whitens the ground where water has risen to the surface and gone back down.

**allus:** always.

**Arizona Rangers:** a group of rangers organized in 1901 to protect the Arizona Territory from outlaws and rustlers so that the Territory could apply for statehood. They were picked from officers, military men, ranchers and cowboys. With maximum company strength of twenty-six men, they covered the entire territory.

**Battle of the Marne:** the name of a battle of World War I that took place near the Marne River in northeastern France in the summer of 1918. It was there the US 3rd Division joined British and French forces to stop the advance of the Germans into France. In two scorching hot days of bloody, hand-to-hand fighting, the US 3rd Division proved themselves to be brave and aggressive and helped to tip the balance of power in favor of the Allied forces.

**batwings:** long chaps (leather leggings the cowboy wears to protect his legs) with big flaps of leather. They usually fasten with rings and snaps.

**beeves:** plural of *beef,* an adult cow, steer or bull raised for its meat.

**border roll:** to spin a gun, with the forefinger slipped through the trigger guard, so that the gun butt is spun back into the palm of the hand, ready to fire.

**border shift:** the throwing of a gun from one hand to the other, catching, cocking and, if need be, firing it without seeming to pause.

**buckaroo:** a cowboy of the West known for their great horsemanship and horse-training techniques. Buckaroos distinguish themselves by their open-crowned hats with short, flat brims, silk scarves, chinks (shorter leather chaps), high-heeled boots, dark wool vests, and white, long-sleeved, button-down shirts.

**buckboard:** an open four-wheeled horse-drawn carriage with the seat or seats mounted on a flexible board between the front and rear axles.

**bucks:** men, especially strong or spirited young men.

**bull's-eye lantern:** a lantern with one or more sides of bulging glass. Dark until it was suddenly switched on by opening its door, it focused its light to some extent.

**bulldogger:** one who bulldogs, to throw a calf or steer by seizing the horns and twisting its neck until the animal loses its balance and falls.

**chaw:** a wad of chewing tobacco.

**chute:** a passage between fences or rails, sometimes narrowing, in which horses or cattle are driven into rodeo arenas, corrals, onto trucks, etc.

**Colt:** a single-action, six-shot cylinder revolver, most commonly available in .45- or .44-caliber versions. It was first manufactured by American inventor Samuel Colt (1814–1862) who revolutionized the firearms industry with the invention of the revolver. The Colt, also known as the Peacemaker, was also made available to civilians. As a reliable, inexpensive and popular handgun among cowboys, it became known as the "cowboy's gun" and a symbol of the Old West.

**concha:** a disk, traditionally of hammered silver and resembling a shell or flower, used as decoration pieces on belts, harnesses, etc.

**Cordilleras:** a mountain system in the West, including the Sierra Nevada, Coast Range, Cascade Range and Rocky Mountains.

**Curly Bill Spin:** used when handing a gun over to someone. As the gun is handed over, butt first, the forefinger is slipped through the trigger guard and the gun butt is spun back into the palm of the hand, ready to fire; named because Curly Bill Graham, a nineteenth century outlaw, used this maneuver to kill a marshal during an attempted arrest.

**'dobe:** short for adobe; building constructed with sun-dried bricks made from clay.

**dogs and children:** referring to the old saying that one cannot fool dogs and children: "If dogs and children like you, then you must be okay."

*dons:* Spanish gentlemen or aristocrats.

**drill:** shoot.

**Ellensburg Rodeo:** Ellensburg is located just east of the Cascade Mountain Range in central Washington. The Ellensburg Rodeo was founded in 1923 by ranchers, farmers, Indians and community-minded citizens with the desire to celebrate a vanishing frontier way of life and to promote their community. Ellensburg lies in the heart of the cattle region and roundup competitions were commonplace with the cowboys of the region.

**fall guy:** an easy victim.

**fanned:** 1. fanning; waving or slapping the hat against a horse's sides while riding a bucker. Using the hat in this manner serves as a balance and when a rider loses his hat, he is usually not long in following it to the ground. 2. fired a series of shots from a single-action revolver by holding the trigger back and successively striking the hammer to the rear with the free hand.

**forked leather:** mounted a saddled horse.

**forty-five** or **.45:** a .45-caliber pistol or revolver.

**Fry, Elizabeth:** (1780–1845) an English prison reformer, social reformer and philanthropist. She was the driving force in the legislation to make the treatment of prisoners more humane.

**ginger:** with great care or caution.

**G-men:** government men; agents of the Federal Bureau of Investigation.

**hackamore:** a halter with reins and a noseband instead of a bit (a metal bar which fits into the horse's mouth and attaches to the reins), used for breaking horses and riding.

**hair pants:** chaps (leather leggings the cowboy wears to protect his legs) made with hair-covered hide.

**half-breed:** a person with parents of different races, usually a white father and Native American mother. The term originated in the East, not the Western frontier.

**hazing:** driving from horseback.

**high-hatting:** treating in a condescending way; showing haughty disdain for.

**hog leg:** another name for the popular Colt revolver also known as the Peacemaker.

**hoof, on the:** a cow that is still alive.

**hoosegow:** a jail.

**hornswoggle:** to trick, deceive or cheat.

**hostler:** a person who takes care of horses, especially at an inn.

**John B.:** Stetson; as the most popular broad-brimmed hat in the West, it became the generic name for *hat*. John B. Stetson was a master hatmaker and founder of the company which has been making Stetsons since 1865.

Not only can the Stetson stand up to a terrific amount of beating, the cowboy's hat has more different uses than any other garment he wears. It keeps the sun out of the eyes and off the neck; it serves as an umbrella; it makes a great fan, which sometimes is needed when building a fire or shunting cattle about; the brim serves as a cup to water oneself, or as a bucket to water the horse or put out the fire.

**lariat:** a long-noosed rope used for catching horses, cattle, etc.; lasso.

**lights:** mental ability, knowledge or understanding.

**livery stable:** a stable that accommodates and looks after horses for their owners.

**lobo:** wolf; one who is regarded as predatory, greedy and fierce.

**locoweed:** any of a number of plants widespread in the mountains of the Western US that make livestock act crazy when they eat them.

**lynch mob:** a group of people who capture and hang someone without legal arrest and trial, because they think the person has committed a crime.

**Major Reno:** Major Marcus Albert Reno (1834–1889); a career military officer in the American Civil War, most noted for his role in the Battle of Little Big Horn, also known as Custer's Last Stand, on June 25, 1876. Custer split his command of the US Cavalry Regiment, numbering 650 men, into 3 battalions. Reno commanded one battalion and crossed the river to attack the southern end of the Indian camp. Realizing a trap had been set, he ordered his men dismounted and went into a defensive formation. Colonel Custer, originally intending to support Reno, attacked the middle of the encampment instead, where he and all 197 of the men in his battalion were killed. Major Reno's battalion of 134 had 36 men killed and 26 wounded.

**Marshall, John:** a book by John Marshall (1755–1835), an American statesman and jurist who shaped American constitutional law and made the Supreme Court a center of power. He was the fourth Chief Justice of the United States, serving from 1801 until his death. He participated in over one thousand Supreme Court decisions and wrote 519 of the opinions himself.

**Morris chair:** an early type of reclining chair from 1866 manufactured by William Morris' firm, Morris & Company. The characteristic feature of the Morris chair is a hinged back, set with two un-upholstered arms, with the reclining angle adjusted through a row of pegs, holes or notches in each arm.

**old saw about "dogs and children":** referring to the old saying that one cannot fool dogs and children: "If dogs and children like you, you must be okay."

**outlaw:** a wild or vicious horse.

**Overland:** Overland Stage; stagecoach line in the mid-nineteenth century that transported mail and passengers.

**papooses:** American Indian infants or very young children.

**physiognomy:** the features of somebody's face, especially when they are used as indicators of that person's character or temperament.

**pinwheel:** a movement or trick with a gun; the gun is held in virtual firing position except that the forefinger is not in the trigger guard. The gun is flipped into the air so that it revolves and the butt drops naturally into the palm of the hand.

**plug:** shoot.

**plugged** *centavo:* a worthless coin. A plugged coin was counterfeit or had a plug of metal removed from the center. *Centavo* is Spanish for a cent or penny.

**plug tabacco:** shredded tobacco leaves pressed into a block.

**polecat:** skunk; a thoroughly contemptible person.

**pulled leather:** grabbed onto the saddle while riding a bucking horse. It shows a lack of skill or courage, or both. A cowboy hates to have to grab the saddle horn to stay on, and most will allow themselves to be thrown off before they will pull leather.

**puncher:** a hired hand who tends cattle and performs other duties on horseback.

**quirt:** a riding whip with a short handle and a braided leather lash.

**repeater watch:** a pocket watch that chimes every one, twelve or twenty-four hours.

**roostered:** drunk.

**roweled:** having used the small, spiked revolving wheels at the ends of spurs, rolled across the horse's side.

**rowels:** the small spiked revolving wheels on the ends of spurs, which are attached to the heels of a rider's boots and used to nudge a horse into going faster.

**running iron:** a branding iron which is not bent into the shape of the mark, but rather requires the user to write the desired brand.

**sap:** dumb guy; a fool.

**Scheherazade:** the female narrator of *The Arabian Nights*, who during one thousand and one adventurous nights saved her life by entertaining her husband, the king, with stories.

**serape:** a long, brightly colored woolen blanket worn as a cloak by some men from Mexico, Central America and South America.

**shucks, wasn't such:** was of little value.

**sombrero:** a Mexican style of hat that was common in the Southwest. It had a high-curved, wide brim, a long, loose chin strap and the crown was dented at the top. Like cowboy hats generally, it kept off the sun and rain, fended off the branches and served as a handy bucket or cup.

**sorrel:** a horse with a reddish-brown coat.

**Stetson:** as the most popular broad-brimmed hat in the West, it became the generic name for *hat*. John B. Stetson was a master hatmaker and founder of the company which has been making Stetsons since 1865. Not only can the Stetson stand up to a terrific amount of beating, the cowboy's hat has more different uses than any other garment he wears. It keeps the sun out of the eyes and off the neck; it serves as an umbrella; it makes a great fan, which sometimes is needed when building a fire or shunting cattle about; the brim serves as a cup to water oneself, or as a bucket to water the horse or put out the fire.

**sunfish:** a way of bucking; the horse throws its middle violently to one side, then the other, so that it seems its shoulder may touch the ground, letting the sunlight hit its belly.

**swap ends:** a movement peculiar to a bronc where he quickly reverses his position, making a complete half-circle in the air.

**thirteenth step:** gallows; traditionally, there are thirteen steps leading up to a gallows.

**Tipperary:** a town of south central Ireland, southwest of Dublin. The song "It's a Long Way to Tipperary" was used as marching music by the British Expeditionary Force in World War I.

**vigilantes:** citizens banded together in the West as vigilance committees, without legal sanction and usually in the absence of effective law enforcement, to take action against men viewed as threats to life and property. The usual pattern of vigilance committees was to grab their enemies (guilty or not), stage a sort of trial and hang them. Their other enemies were then likely to get out of town.

**waddies:** cowboys, especially those who drift from ranch to ranch and help out in busy times. In the spring and fall when some ranches were short-handed, they took on anyone who was able to ride a horse and used him for a week or so; hence the word *waddy,* derived from *wadding*—anything to fill in. Some cowmen used the word to mean a cattle rustler; later it was applied to any cowboy.

**whippersnapper:** an impertinent young person, usually a young man, who lacks proper respect for the older generation; a youngster with an excess of both ambition and impertinence.

**Winchester:** an early family of repeating rifles, a single-barreled rifle containing multiple rounds of ammunition. Manufactured by the Winchester Repeating Arms Company, it was widely used in the US during the latter half of the nineteenth century. The 1873 model is often called "the gun that won the West" for its immense popularity at that time, as well as its use in fictional Westerns.

**ye:** you.

L. Ron Hubbard
in the Golden Age
of Pulp Fiction

*In writing an adventure story
a writer has to know that he is adventuring
for a lot of people who cannot.
The writer has to take them here and there
about the globe and show them
excitement and love and realism.
As long as that writer is living the part of an
adventurer when he is hammering
the keys, he is succeeding with his story.*

*Adventuring is a state of mind.
If you adventure through life, you have a
good chance to be a success on paper.*

*Adventure doesn't mean globe-trotting,
exactly, and it doesn't mean great deeds.
Adventuring is like art.
You have to live it to make it real.*

—*L. RON HUBBARD*

# L. Ron Hubbard
# and American
# Pulp Fiction

BORN March 13, 1911, L. Ron Hubbard lived a life at least as expansive as the stories with which he enthralled a hundred million readers through a fifty-year career.

Originally hailing from Tilden, Nebraska, he spent his formative years in a classically rugged Montana, replete with the cowpunchers, lawmen and desperadoes who would later people his Wild West adventures. And lest anyone imagine those adventures were drawn from vicarious experience, he was not only breaking broncs at a tender age, he was also among the few whites ever admitted into Blackfoot society as a bona fide blood brother. While if only to round out an otherwise rough and tumble youth, his mother was that rarity of her time—a thoroughly educated woman—who introduced her son to the classics of Occidental literature even before his seventh birthday.

But as any dedicated L. Ron Hubbard reader will attest, his world extended far beyond Montana. In point of fact, and as the son of a United States naval officer, by the age of eighteen he had traveled over a quarter of a million miles. Included therein were three Pacific crossings to a then still mysterious Asia, where he ran with the likes of Her British Majesty's agent-in-place

*L. Ron Hubbard, left, at Congressional Airport, Washington, DC, 1931, with members of George Washington University flying club.*

for North China, and the last in the line of Royal Magicians from the court of Kublai Khan. For the record, L. Ron Hubbard was also among the first Westerners to gain admittance to forbidden Tibetan monasteries below Manchuria, and his photographs of China's Great Wall long graced American geography texts.

Upon his return to the United States and a hasty completion of his interrupted high school education, the young Ron Hubbard entered George Washington University. There, as fans of his aerial adventures may have heard, he earned his wings as a pioneering barnstormer at the dawn of American aviation. He also earned a place in free-flight record books for the longest sustained flight above Chicago. Moreover, as a roving reporter for *Sportsman Pilot* (featuring his first professionally penned articles), he further helped inspire a generation of pilots who would take America to world airpower.

Immediately beyond his sophomore year, Ron embarked on the first of his famed ethnological expeditions, initially to then untrammeled Caribbean shores (descriptions of which would later fill a whole series of West Indies mystery-thrillers). That the Puerto Rican interior would also figure into the future of Ron Hubbard stories was likewise no accident. For in addition to cultural studies of the island, a 1932–33

LRH expedition is rightly remembered as conducting the first complete mineralogical survey of a Puerto Rico under United States jurisdiction.

There was many another adventure along this vein: As a lifetime member of the famed Explorers Club, L. Ron Hubbard charted North Pacific waters with the first shipboard radio direction finder, and so pioneered a long-range navigation system universally employed until the late twentieth century. While not to put too fine an edge on it, he also held a rare Master Mariner's license to pilot any vessel, of any tonnage in any ocean.

Yet lest we stray too far afield, there is an LRH note at this juncture in his saga, and it reads in part:

*"I started out writing for the pulps, writing the best I knew, writing for every mag on the stands, slanting as well as I could."*

To which one might add: His earliest submissions date from the summer of 1934, and included tales drawn from true-to-life Asian adventures, with characters roughly modeled on British/American intelligence operatives he had known in Shanghai. His early Westerns were similarly peppered with details drawn from personal

*Capt. L. Ron Hubbard in Ketchikan, Alaska, 1940, on his Alaskan Radio Experimental Expedition, the first of three voyages conducted under the Explorers Club flag.*

experience. Although therein lay a first hard lesson from the often cruel world of the pulps. His first Westerns were soundly rejected as lacking the authenticity of a Max Brand yarn (a particularly frustrating comment given L. Ron Hubbard's Westerns came straight from his Montana homeland, while Max Brand was a mediocre New York poet named Frederick Schiller Faust, who turned out implausible six-shooter tales from the terrace of an Italian villa).

Nevertheless, and needless to say, L. Ron Hubbard persevered and soon earned a reputation as among the most publishable names in pulp fiction, with a ninety percent placement rate of first-draft manuscripts. He was also among the most prolific, averaging between seventy and a hundred thousand words a month. Hence the rumors that L. Ron Hubbard had redesigned a typewriter for faster keyboard action and pounded out manuscripts on a continuous roll of butcher paper to save the precious seconds it took to insert a single sheet of paper into manual typewriters of the day.

That all L. Ron Hubbard stories did not run beneath said byline is yet another aspect of pulp fiction lore. That is, as publishers periodically rejected manuscripts from top-drawer authors if only to avoid paying top dollar, L. Ron Hubbard and company just as frequently replied with submissions under various pseudonyms. In Ron's case, the

## A MAN OF MANY NAMES

*Between 1934 and 1950, L. Ron Hubbard authored more than fifteen million words of fiction in more than two hundred classic publications. To supply his fans and editors with stories across an array of genres and pulp titles, he adopted fifteen pseudonyms in addition to his already renowned L. Ron Hubbard byline.*

*Winchester Remington Colt*
*Lt. Jonathan Daly*
*Capt. Charles Gordon*
*Capt. L. Ron Hubbard*
*Bernard Hubbel*
*Michael Keith*
*Rene Lafayette*
*Legionnaire 148*
*Legionnaire 14830*
*Ken Martin*
*Scott Morgan*
*Lt. Scott Morgan*
*Kurt von Rachen*
*Barry Randolph*
*Capt. Humbert Reynolds*

list included: Rene Lafayette, Captain Charles Gordon, Lt. Scott Morgan and the notorious Kurt von Rachen—supposedly on the lam for a murder rap, while hammering out two-fisted prose in Argentina. The point: While L. Ron Hubbard as Ken Martin spun stories of Southeast Asian intrigue, LRH as Barry Randolph authored tales of romance on the Western range—which, stretching between a dozen genres is how he came to stand among the two hundred elite authors providing close to a million tales through the glory days of American Pulp Fiction.

*L. Ron Hubbard, circa 1930, at the outset of a literary career that would finally span half a century.*

In evidence of exactly that, by 1936 L. Ron Hubbard was literally leading pulp fiction's elite as president of New York's American Fiction Guild. Members included a veritable pulp hall of fame: Lester "Doc Savage" Dent, Walter "The Shadow" Gibson, and the legendary Dashiell Hammett—to cite but a few.

Also in evidence of just where L. Ron Hubbard stood within his first two years on the American pulp circuit: By the spring of 1937, he was ensconced in Hollywood, adopting a Caribbean thriller for Columbia Pictures, remembered today as *The Secret of Treasure Island*. Comprising fifteen thirty-minute episodes, the L. Ron Hubbard screenplay led to the most profitable matinée serial in Hollywood history. In accord with Hollywood culture, he was thereafter continually called upon

*The 1937* Secret of Treasure Island, *a fifteen-episode serial adapted for the screen by L. Ron Hubbard from his novel,* Murder at Pirate Castle.

to rewrite/doctor scripts—most famously for long-time friend and fellow adventurer Clark Gable.

In the interim—and herein lies another distinctive chapter of the L. Ron Hubbard story—he continually worked to open Pulp Kingdom gates to up-and-coming authors. Or, for that matter, anyone who wished to write. It was a fairly unconventional stance, as markets were already thin and competition razor sharp. But the fact remains, it was an L. Ron Hubbard hallmark that he vehemently lobbied on behalf of young authors—regularly supplying instructional articles to trade journals, guest-lecturing to short story classes at George Washington University and Harvard, and even founding his own creative writing competition. It was established in 1940, dubbed the Golden Pen, and guaranteed winners both New York representation and publication in *Argosy*.

But it was John W. Campbell Jr.'s *Astounding Science Fiction* that finally proved the most memorable LRH vehicle. While every fan of L. Ron Hubbard's galactic epics undoubtedly knows the story, it nonetheless bears repeating: By late 1938, the pulp publishing magnate of Street & Smith was determined to revamp *Astounding Science Fiction* for broader readership. In particular, senior editorial director F. Orlin Tremaine called for stories with a stronger *human element*. When acting editor John W. Campbell balked, preferring his spaceship-driven tales, Tremaine enlisted Hubbard. Hubbard, in turn, replied with the genre's first truly *character-driven* works, wherein heroes are pitted not against bug-eyed monsters but the mystery and majesty of deep space itself—and thus was launched the Golden Age of Science Fiction.

The names alone are enough to quicken the pulse of any science fiction aficionado, including LRH friend and protégé, Robert Heinlein, Isaac Asimov, A. E. van Vogt and Ray Bradbury. Moreover, when coupled with LRH stories of fantasy, we further come to what's rightly been described as the foundation of every modern tale of horror: L. Ron Hubbard's immortal *Fear.* It was rightly proclaimed by Stephen King as one of the very few works to genuinely warrant that overworked term "classic"—as in: *"This is a classic tale of creeping, surreal menace and horror. . . . This is one of the really, really good ones."*

To accommodate the greater body of L. Ron Hubbard fantasies, Street & Smith inaugurated *Unknown*—a classic pulp if there ever was one, and wherein readers were soon thrilling to the likes of *Typewriter in the Sky* and *Slaves of Sleep* of which Frederik Pohl would declare: *"There are bits and pieces from Ron's work that became part of the language in ways that very few other writers managed."*

*L. Ron Hubbard, 1948, among fellow science fiction luminaries at the World Science Fiction Convention in Toronto.*

And, indeed, at J. W. Campbell Jr.'s insistence, Ron was regularly drawing on themes from the Arabian Nights and

145

so introducing readers to a world of genies, jinn, Aladdin and Sinbad—all of which, of course, continue to float through cultural mythology to this day.

At least as influential in terms of post-apocalypse stories was L. Ron Hubbard's 1940 *Final Blackout*. Generally acclaimed as the finest anti-war novel of the decade and among the ten best works of the genre ever authored—here, too, was a tale that would live on in ways few other writers imagined.

Hence, the later Robert Heinlein verdict: "Final Blackout *is as perfect a piece of science fiction as has ever been written.*"

Like many another who both lived and wrote American pulp adventure, the war proved a tragic end to Ron's sojourn in the pulps. He served with distinction in four theaters and was highly decorated

*Portland, Oregon, 1943; L. Ron Hubbard, captain of the US Navy subchaser PC 815.*

for commanding corvettes in the North Pacific. He was also grievously wounded in combat, lost many a close friend and colleague and thus resolved to say farewell to pulp fiction and devote himself to what it had supported these many years—namely, his serious research.

But in no way was the LRH literary saga at an end, for as he wrote some thirty years later, in 1980:

*"Recently there came a period when I had little to do. This was novel in a life so crammed with busy years, and I decided to amuse myself by writing a novel that was* pure *science fiction."*

That work was *Battlefield Earth: A Saga of the Year 3000*. It was an immediate *New York Times* bestseller and, in fact, the first international science fiction blockbuster in decades. It was not, however, L. Ron Hubbard's magnum opus, as that distinction is generally reserved for his next and final work: The 1.2 million word *Mission Earth*.

> **Final Blackout** *is as perfect a piece of science fiction as has ever been written.*
>
> —Robert Heinlein

How he managed those 1.2 million words in just over twelve months is yet another piece of the L. Ron Hubbard legend. But the fact remains, he did indeed author a ten-volume *dekalogy* that lives in publishing history for the fact that each and every volume of the series was also a *New York Times* bestseller.

Moreover, as subsequent generations discovered L. Ron Hubbard through republished works and novelizations of his screenplays, the mere fact of his name on a cover signaled an international bestseller. . . . Until, to date, sales of his works exceed hundreds of millions, and he otherwise remains among the most enduring and widely read authors in literary history. Although as a final word on the tales of L. Ron Hubbard, perhaps it's enough to simply reiterate what editors told readers in the glory days of American Pulp Fiction:

*He writes the way he does, brothers, because he's been there, seen it and done it!*

# THE STORIES FROM THE GOLDEN AGE

Your ticket to adventure starts here with the Stories from
the Golden Age collection by master storyteller L. Ron Hubbard.
These gripping tales are set in a kaleidoscope of exotic locales and brim
with fascinating characters, including some of the
most vile villains, dangerous dames and brazen heroes
you'll ever get to meet.

The entire collection of over one hundred and fifty stories is being
released in a series of eighty books and audiobooks.
For an up-to-date listing of available titles,
go to www.goldenagestories.com.

## AIR ADVENTURE

## FAR-FLUNG ADVENTURE

## SEA ADVENTURE

## TALES FROM THE ORIENT

## MYSTERY

151

## FANTASY

## SCIENCE FICTION